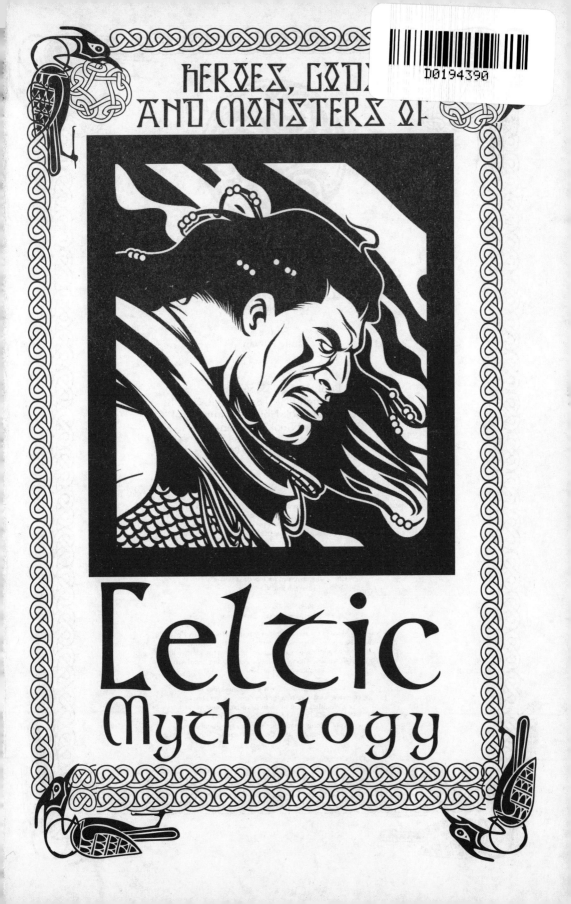

HEROES, GODS
AND MONSTERS OF

Celtic
Mythology

Cover artwork by
Mike Ray

Created and Designed By
David Salariya

Editor
Jamie Pitman

Published by **S** SCRIBO
25 Marlborough Place, Brighton BN1 1UB
A division of Book House, an imprint of
The Salariya Book Company Ltd.

ISBN 978-1-910706-04-6

1 3 5 7 9 8 6 4 2

A CIP catalogue record for this book is available
from the British Library.

Printed and bound in India.
Printed on paper from sustainable sources.

Visit our website at **www.book-house.com**
or go to **www.salariya.com** for **free** electronic versions of:
You Wouldn't Want to be an Egyptian Mummy!
You Wouldn't Want to be a Roman Gladiator!
Avoid Joining Shackleton's Polar Expedition!
Avoid Sailing on a 19th-Century Whaling Ship!

HEROES, GODS AND MONSTERS OF

Celtic Mythology

by

Fiona Macdonald

ILLUSTRATED BY

Eoin Coveney

SCRIBO

THE CELTIC
WORLD
THRILLED
AND
SHIVERED
WITH
PROMISE,
POSSIBILITY
AND DANGER

INTRODUCTION

Magic Kingdoms

Prepare to enter a land full of adventure, magic and mystery.

The Celtic world was an enchanted place, where gods fought demons and monsters, birds and animals talked to humans, and men and women travelled through time or visited magic kingdoms. Every rock and tree and river was alive with

its own good, or evil, spirit. Nothing was what it seemed to be; the gods, and human heroes, loved trickery and disguises. The Celtic world thrilled and shivered with promise, possibility, love – and danger.

This book contains a collection of Celtic myths and legends from Ireland, Wales, Scotland, England, the Isle of Man, and Brittany in north-western France. Like traditional stories from other lands, they have all been told countless times before in many different ways. They have also inspired great music and paintings, provided plots for writers and film-makers, and been turned into fantasy re-enactments, comic books, and computer games.

Try retelling your favourite story from this book in your own words, or use it to help you make your own magic creation!

Who were the Celts?

The Celts lived in northern Europe from around 800 BC to AD 400. They belonged to many different tribes and nations, but they all spoke closely related languages and shared a similar way of life. They believed in the same family of gods and nature-spirits, honoured brave, reckless heroes, and followed proud warrior kings and queens who claimed religious and magical powers.

Most Celtic families made a living as farmers. They were free and independent but owed loyalty to their clan chief and high king. There were also Celtic traders and craft-workers living in fortress towns, and thousands of Celtic slaves.

Celtic kings and chiefs were rich enough to ride fine horses and chariots, and wear weapons and jewellery decorated with swirling, magical designs. They had druids (priests) to say prayers and make sacrifices,

linking everyday Celtic life with the dreamy, dangerous Otherworld of gods and spirits. They paid bards (poets and music-makers) to sing the praises of heroes and record each tribe's history, myths and legends.

'Being Celtic' meant taking part in this rich civilisation. The Celts were not an ethnic group, but rather peoples with a shared lifestyle. They were descended from the first farmers in northern Europe, who began planting crops and rearing animals around 4000 BC. New DNA evidence links some Celts to hunters and gatherers who arrived in northern Europe at the end of the last Ice Age, over 10,000 years ago.

Celtic civilisation developed slowly from around 1500 BC, when craft-workers learned how to make armour and helmets from bronze (a mixture of copper and tin, which were traded long-distance by prehistoric peoples).

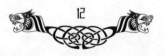

By around 800 BC, their descendants had found out how to make weapons and tools from harder, stronger iron. They also built heavy, horse-drawn wagons, buried their leaders with splendid treasures, and created their first art in a typically Celtic style.

Celtic peoples were most powerful from around 500 BC. By then, they were making better weapons and finer metalwork, and building fast, light chariots for warriors to ride into battle. After around 200 BC, Celtic lands were attacked by Roman armies and German tribes. By AD 100 the Celts had almost all been defeated. But Celtic culture survived in remote parts of Europe, such as Ireland and Brittany, for another 1,000 years.

CELTIC LANDS

This map shows where the stories in this book first originated.

SCOTLAND
12, 13

IRELAND
1, 2, 3, 6,
7, 10

ISLE OF
MAN
15

WALES
4, 5, 9

EAST
ANGLIA
14

BRITTANY
8, 11, 16

Timeline of Celtic peoples

c. 10,000–8000 BC
Hunter-gatherers move into northern Europe at the end of the last Ice age.

c. 4000 BC
First farmers in northern Europe.

c. 3000–1000 BC
Farming kings and communities build huge stone circles and tombs.

c. 1500–800 BC
Bronze Age – skilled craft-workers make bronze armour and weapons.

c. 800–500 BC
Hallstatt Era – first clearly Celtic culture: rich kings and queens, iron weapons, jewellery, international trade.

c. 500–200 BC
La Tène era – peak of Celtic power. Warriors drive fast chariots; Celts attack rich neighbouring lands; many fine crafts.

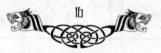

c. 200–AD 100
Celtic lands invaded and almost completely conquered by Roman and German tribes.

c. AD 500–1000
Most Celts become Christians, but artists working for the Church preserve and continue Celtic traditions. Writers in Celtic lands collect and preserve old Celtic myths and legends.

How do we know?

Celtic peoples did not read and write or keep written records. But we know about their lives, ideas and beliefs from three very different sources.

Buried treasures

The Celts believed in life after death, so they buried men, women and children with goods that they might need for their new life in the Otherworld. The graves of rich people tell us the most, but even poor graves can be revealing. Rich kings and queens were laid to rest with their weapons, jewellery, horses, chariots, and drinking cups, ready for fighting and feasting. Many were also buried with huge cauldrons – for mixing wine, and for magic or religious rituals.

Poor peoples' graves hold few treasures, but important information. For example, children were sometimes buried with shoes several sizes too big; this tells us that their parents must have expected them to go on growing in the Otherworld. Some old women, who were

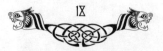

probably believed to have been witches, had their jawbones removed before burial, possibly to stop them casting spells or making curses.

Enemy observers

From around 500 BC, the Celts traded and fought against Greeks and Romans, who could read and write. Greek and Roman authors have left eye-witness descriptions of Celtic people, but these have to be read with caution. For example, the Greeks were the first to record a name for the Celts – Keltoi – though we don't know if Celts used this term.

Roman army commanders admired the bravery of Celtic warriors, but treated them as enemies. They wrote that the Celts were wild, dangerous and uncivilised. They also disapproved of Celtic religious beliefs, possibly because they didn't understand them properly.

Stories with meanings

Myths are stories that explain things people can't describe in other ways. They explain why a king lost a war, why men and women die for love, or why the sun shines in the sky. Legends are stories linked to a particular place or person. They may be completely imaginary, or contain true histories of the distant past mixed with newly invented details.

For many centuries, Celtic myths and legends were memorised and passed on by word of mouth, from generation to generation. But, after around AD 500, Christian monks in Celtic lands began to collect these ancient stories and write them down. For reasons still unknown today the first texts have all vanished, but later copies survive dating from around AD 1200. Thanks to them, we can still enjoy Celtic myths today.

European languages, especially English, still contain many Celtic words, such as 'avon' (river), or 'scone' (small round cake). Parents still choose Celtic names for their children,

such as Brian or Hugh or Bridget or Rhiannon. And thousands of people in Ireland, Scotland, Wales and Brittany still speak Celtic languages.

A note on names

The stories in this book come from different parts of the Celtic world: Ireland, Wales, Scotland, Brittany (in France) and the Isle of Man. People living in those lands all spoke Celtic languages, but each in their own way. So the same word or the same name, spoken by different Celtic people, might sound slightly different. For example, the name 'Janet' is Seonaid [Shonn-idge] in Scottish Gaelic, but in Irish Gaelic it is Sinead [Shin-aid].

Over the centuries, writers and scholars have also used many different ways of translating the sounds of Celtic words and names into the common sounds of English. This means that you will often find the names of the same heroes and monsters from Celtic myths and legends spelled in different ways.

This doesn't really matter though, because although the spellings of some Celtic names look rather difficult at first sight, most are really quite easy to say. At the end of this book is an index of characters and

pronunciations. It is only a rough guide to pronunciation, but it should help. Better still, if you can find someone who has one of these Celtic names, or speaks a Celtic language, ask them, and learn!

Eoghan?

Eoin?   *Ewen?*

Euan?

Owen?

Youenn?

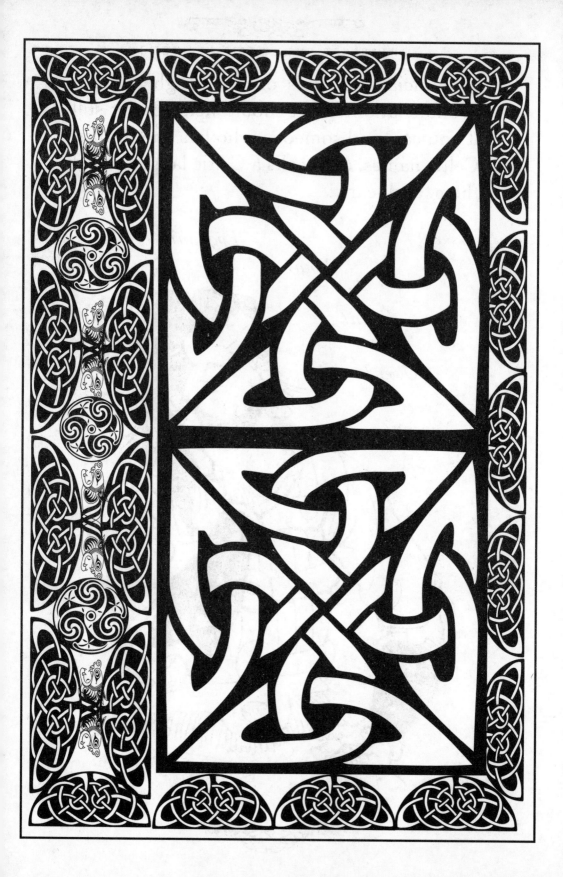

SWIFT AND SURE LIKE AN ARROW, HIS EYE KEEN AND SHARP AS A NEEDLE, FINTAN THE HAWK WATCHED AND WAITED

CHAPTER 1

Fintan the Salmon

own in the depths of the sea, splashing in the sunlit rivers, Fintan the Salmon watched and waited. High in the cold, bright sky, crouched over bloody carcasses, Fintan the Eagle watched and waited. Swift and sure like an arrow, his eye keen and sharp as a needle, Fintan the Hawk watched and waited.

Fintan the magician. Fintan the shape-shifter. Fintan, the last man left alive in Ireland after the Flood at the very Start of the World. Transforming himself into many different creatures, Fintan waited and watched while Ireland's destiny passed before his eyes.

This is what he saw: After Fintan's people were swept away in a flood, Ireland was empty. Empty, that is, apart from Fomorians, demons who had been there since time began. Fintan's drowned family had been the first people in Ireland. Now he saw new arrivals land on Ireland's rocky beaches. But who among them would survive?

First came Partholon and his family, and three druids. All died of plague. Next came Nemed [Nemm-eth] and his tribe. They cleared the forests and dug great lakes, but they were killed by the Fomorians.

After them, the Fir Bholg [Fear Volg] and their friends arrived. They settled, and lived as farmers. But they were only ordinary human beings – unlike the next invaders.

It was magical May Day, the feast of Bright Fire, when the Tuatha De Danann [Tootha Day Dann-ann; People of the Goddess] mysteriously appeared. Did they

ride on the wind, or shimmer out of the sunlight, or flicker from the flames of spring bonfires? Strange and supernatural, they shared the powers of Danu [Dan-oo], the Great Mother. They were skilled in fighting, magic and religion. Their chiefs were mortal warriors and immortal gods.

The Tuatha De Danann brought four magic talismans with them to Ireland (objects believed to have magic or protective powers), to help them win, and keep, power. The Stone of Fal cried out with joy when touched by a lawful king, but stayed silent for impostors; the glowing, white-hot Spear of Light brought victory to any warrior; no enemy could escape the Sword of Nuada [Noo-ah-da], that hunted down victims and murdered them; and no-one was ever hungry after eating from the bottomless Cauldron of the Good God, the Daghda [Dah-da].

The Fir Bholg were horrified. How could they defend their fields and farms against such superhuman enemies? But they had no choice. Knowing that they were doomed to defeat, they declared war on the invaders.

It was a fierce battle, and a brave but terrible one. As they had feared, the Fir Bholg

were all slaughtered. But the Tuatha De Danann also suffered badly. Nuada, their god-king, lost his strong right arm. His days as a warrior were over.

Nuada had to hand over his crown. The law said each king should be perfect, and in no way mutilated. In his place the Tuatha De Danann chose the strongest man in Ireland – Bres [Bresh], a Fomorian warrior.

Bres was a dreadful ruler. He was cruel and untrustworthy, spiteful and mean, and delighted in doing harm. But, because Bres was a demon, it was difficult for anyone, even the Tuatha De Danann, to fight against him and win.

At last they tricked Bres, and disgraced him. Everyone mocked him, and refused to respect him or obey his orders. The shame was so great that Bres was forced to run away, and Nuada became king once more. His best metalworkers made him a silver arm to replace the one he had lost in battle.

The Fomorians were furious, ashamed and insulted. They all felt the disgrace of Bres, their king. So they called on their greatest champion to lead the fight against the Tuatha De Danann. His name? Balor [Bahlor]. His

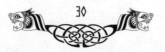

size? Gigantic. Balor the Giant. Balor with the Evil Eye!

Like almost all Fomorians, Balor was horribly ugly. He had only one eye, huge and angry. Its lid was so heavy that it needed four strong men to heave it up and hold it open. The bloodshot, leering, eyeball dripped deadly poison, and its lashes were spiky, like thorns. A single glance from it could kill a man where he stood.

Who could fight against this fearsome monster? Only one hero, the bright and shining Lugh [Lou]. Lord of the Sunrise, Lugh wore the stars of the Milky Way as a necklace, and carried a rainbow over his arm. Lugh was the champion of the Tuatha De Danann, but had Fomorian blood as well. Lugh's birth made sure that an old curse could come true: that Balor would be killed by his grandson.

Long ago, Balor had a daughter. She was as sweet and kind as great big Balor was ugly, but Balor kept her hidden away. He was determined that she would never meet a man or give birth to children. That way, Balor hoped he could defeat the curse, and live for ever.

But Kian [Kee-an], a hero from the Tuatha De Danann, decided that evil Balor must die. So, secretly, he tracked Balor's daughter down to the cave where she was hidden, and they soon fell in love.

When the Fomorians discovered this, they chased and killed Kian. But it was too late! Balor's daughter was already the mother of three beautiful sons. Appalled and raging, Balor threw the babies into the sea, certain that they would drown. But one swam ashore. It was Lugh.

The war-trumpets made a fearsome sound, like wild beasts yelling and shrieking. The war-horses stamped. The warriors rattled their shields in fury. Lugh the Champion stood at the head of his men, shouting defiance at the Fomorians. Scornfully, they roared back: Lugh's death was coming to meet him!

Charge! The horsemen and chariots raced ahead, and the armies clashed with a sound like thunder.

Then closer, closer, closer... giant footsteps made the ground tremble. A vast shadow blotted out the sun: Balor was marching towards them!

Slowly, Balor lumbered to the top of the nearest hill. From there, he could look down on Lugh's army. His four companions – the men who guided him and opened his eye – climbed up on to his shoulders, grimly.

Lugh hid, but the dark light flooding from Balor's evil eye killed all his men in an instant. Safe behind a rock, Lugh shuddered and staggered and fell, as if he'd been struck by lightning.

The four companions climbed up again. But now Lugh was ready and waiting. Riding his magic horse that ran faster than the wind, he flew straight for Balor. With his rainbow sling, Lugh hurled a killer stone straight into Balor's eye. The bloody eyeball shuddered, twisted – and was pushed right through the back of Balor's head!

Now all the Fomorians lay dead on the ground behind Balor. His evil eye had killed them as he lay dying. Lugh was the triumphant champion.

For centuries, the Tuatha De Danann lived in Ireland alone, hunting, farming and feasting. But then Fintan the Salmon, still watching, still waiting, saw Ireland's last invaders approaching. These were the Gaels,

the Celts' ancestors. They were men and women, not gods, with human hopes and fears and weaknesses. They were brave warriors, keen to fight, but they could never win against the Tuatha de Danaan.

At last both sides agreed to make peace. The Gaels would breathe the air and farm the soil of Ireland. The Tuatha De Danann would live in Ireland too, but out of sight, in the Otherworld. And their magic powers would stay with them for ever, to help or harm humans.

There is no map to show where the Otherworld is, and no road leading to it. The ancient Celts believed the entrance was through green hollow hills they called *sidhe* [shee]. Today, you may perhaps glimpse it just when you least expect it, in shifting shadows or flickering sunlight, or under the restless waves of the sea. If Celtic myths are to be believed, it is wonderful and terrible, deathless and deadly. Enter it at your peril.

SETANTA
WAS
CLEARLY
NOT
LIKE
OTHER
BOYS

CHAPTER 2

Ulster's Hero

Fedelma the druid gazed dreamily into the future: 'I see it bloodstained; I see it red!' she cried out. 'I see a fair man who will perform weapon-feats, with many a wound in his flesh. A hero's light is on his brow…'[1]

The brave deeds of Cu Chulainn [Coo-shull-in],

1. From a translation by Lady Gregory, found here: http://www.ucc.ie/celt/published/T301012/index.html

Ulster's hero, are countless. Who can tell all his adventures? His life was short – only 27 years on this earth – but his fame and glory live forever.

Who can describe Cu Chulainn's strength as he fought 100 warriors at once, or split a raging ogre's head in pieces? Or say how he ripped the heart from the Lake Monster, and chased a murderous giant back to its grisly home beneath the sea? Who knows how he tore treacherous ghosts to shreds, barehanded, or tamed a witch by trickery?

Who could equal Cu Chulainn's courage as he dared insult the deadly war-goddess, Morrigan? And who but he would venture into the Otherworld's deepest pits to meet sharp-horned, triple-tailed, flesh-eating snakes – and dead men's heads, still talking, stuck on bloody spears?

All Ulster trembled at the power of Cu Chulainn's magic when he brandished the Gae Bolga – his barbed spear cursed by witches. No foe ever recovered from that weapon's wounds! No other man could wear his enchanted helmet, a gift from the sea-god, Manannan, or the wondrous cloak that made him invisible. And only he could call on Lugh,

the god of warriors, to heal his battle-injuries and make him strong again.

Who else in Ireland could balance on the sharp tip of an upturned spear? Or leap, like a salmon, over enemies' heads, and hover high above the battlefield? Or swim more swiftly than fish, and run faster than any deer?

And who, apart from Cu Chulainn's trusty charioteer, could drive his wild war-horses, so closely-linked with the hero that they were born on the same day as him?

And who could hear the horses' sad, sad whinnying, warnings of future dangers, and see them weep tears of blood when they knew death was approaching?

No-one. In a land of brave men, and in an age of great heroes, there were none which could be compared to Cu Chulainn.

To begin at the beginning.....

Dechtire [Deck-tir–a], an Ulster princess, gave birth to a baby in a snowstorm. The baby's father was a god in disguise, or an Irish king, or a warrior. No-one knows that, either. The baby's name was Setanta, and the greatest men in Ulster taught him poetry, wisdom, warfare – and, perhaps most importantly, magic.

From childhood, Setanta was clearly not the same as other boys. The gods had created him for an especially superhuman future. He was extremely tall, enormously strong and extraordinarily handsome. Seven bright pupils glowed in each eye, like jewels on a magic cauldron. He had seven skilful fingers on each huge hand, and seven toes on each nimble foot.

His long, flowing, hair was black at the roots, then became russet-red, then was tipped with gold. He wrapped himself in a blood-red cloak, and war-painted his cheeks with four bright colours. He wore a hundred strings of jewelled beads on his head, and a hundred gold necklaces. At times, a strange glow would flicker over

his face, silvery and sinister, like a glimpse of moonlight.

Setanta's first adventure gave him his warrior name. This is how it happened. At just seven years old, he ran away to join boys fighting for the King of Ulster. To prove his worth, he quarrelled, fought and defeated each of them before making his way, at nightfall, to the house where the king was busy feasting.

This house belonged to a blacksmith, named Culann [Coo-lan], and he owned a savage guard-dog. Each night, he set it free to patrol the land around his home. He did not know that Setanta was approaching.

The dog did its duty. With bared fangs and a blood-curdling growl, it hurled itself towards the stranger. But with just one hand, Setanta picked it up and smashed it to its death against a stone pillar.

At first, Culann could not believe what he had seen, then he howled with grief and fury. 'But I will protect you instead of that dog!' Setanta said. 'Put your trust in me.'

A sudden voice rang out of the dark. It was Cathbad [Cuthbert], the king's druid. 'Now you have a new name and a new task,

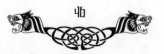

young man. You are Cu Chulainn – Culann's Hound – Guardian of Ireland!'

Cu Chulainn stayed with Culann for a while, but he dreamed of greater adventures. As Fedelma foretold, a brave and bloodstained future lay ahead. He was eager to join it.

Then Cu Chulainn heard Cathbad make a solemn prophecy: 'Any man who becomes a warrior this day will be sure of fame and glory…'

Cu Chulainn ran straight to find the king. 'My lord, you must help me,' he cried. 'Please give me weapons and armour today! You have to make me one of your warriors!'

Back at the holy place, Cathbad went on chanting: 'Yes, that man will be glorious indeed, but his time on earth will be fleeting.'

But Cu Chulainn and the king, out looking for weapons, did not hear these portentous words.

Fifteen times, Cu Chulainn tried to pick up a spear in his huge hands. Fifteen times he tried to swing a sword through the air. But he was far too big, too fierce and too strong. Each weapon bent and crumpled as he touched it.

Eventually, all the swords and spears had been tried, except for the king's own royal weapons. They were magnificent – tremendously tough, strong and true, and decorated with magic designs. At last! They seemed to leap into Cu Chulainn's hands, as if they recognised their rightful owner.

'Welcome, warrior!' said the king. 'Welcome to my army!'

The king also gave Cu Chulainn his deadly horse-drawn war-chariot. It had sharp blades fixed to each wheel to mow men down like grass.

Now that Cu Chulainn was ready, he lost no time in his attacks. His first target was the boastful Three Sons of Nechtan [Neck-tan], who lived further south in Ireland. Foolishly, they claimed to have killed more than half the fighting men of Ulster. Now it was their turn to leave this world.

Cu Chulainn returned from this battle – and many others – in a supernatural frenzy. Transformed from a boy, he became a raging monster, completely out of control. His body spun round within his skin so that his knees and feet faced backwards. His long hair stood on end, each strand tipped with blood or fire. His muscles swelled to an enormous size; his jaws gaped and foamed and spluttered. Black blood gushed from the top of his head, fire belched from his mouth; one eye sank deep inside his skull, the other bulged horrendously. Sometimes, his battle-fury boiled so fiercely that he could no longer tell friends from enemies. It took three huge vats of icy water to quench his burning anger.

Cu Chulainn's superhuman strength and amazing good looks (when he was not raging) brought great praise, but also jealousy. 'Don't

boast!' his rivals said. 'And stay away from our wives and daughters, or we'll kill you!'

'You still have much to learn!', they added. 'You must go to Scathach [Scah-hah], the Wise One.'

Witch, warrior, prophet, teacher – Scathach was pitiless and terrifying. She ran a school for young heroes in wild Alba (now Scotland). Many brave boys died there, but Cu Chulainn survived. He helped save Scathach in a battle, and later had a son with her sister.

Scathach rewarded Cu Chulainn with magic gifts to help him fight. But, like Fedelma and Cathbad, she saw blood and death waiting for him.

Death, or at least his own, was very far from Cu Chulainn's mind when he returned to the king's court in Ulster. He found himself with a lot of work to do, because all the adult warriors there had been cursed!

The curse was caused by the foolish pride of one old Ulster hero. He boasted that Macha [Mock-ah], his young wife from the Otherworld, could run faster than the king's horses. Macha was due to give birth to twins, but now she had to prove her speed in

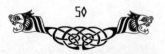

running. She won the race, but died – leaving behind her a vicious curse...

Macha's curse made all adult Ulstermen as weak as a woman after childbirth. It struck each time any danger threatened them, and lasted five days and four nights. Just 17 years old and filled with magic power, only Cu Chulainn escaped it.

Now deadly danger was approaching fast! Queen Medb [Maeve] of Connacht, Ulster's enemy, was leading what was to be known as the great Cattle Raid of Cooley, all because of an enchanted bull.

Single-handed, until the curse passed, Cu Chulainn must defend the kingdom!

Like Cu Chulainn himself, Medb was Otherworldly and superhuman. She was a cunning goddess, a malicious warrior and a jealous wife. Fedelma had warned her that Cu Chulainn would slaughter her army, but she refused to surrender or feel fear. She was determined to attack Ulster, over and over and over again.

This war started because Medb wanted – oh! so much – the enchanted Brown Bull of Ulster. It was the biggest, most beautiful bull in the world, far better than any beast on her

husband's farms. Fifty boys could ride on its back, and it could understand human speech. She would pay any price to purchase it. Or, if she had to, she would steal it.

When the Brown Bull's owner heard about Medb's plans, he hid the Bull far out of sight. Furious at being thwarted, Medb invaded Ulster.

Great, brave and glorious were the battles Cu Chulainn fought against Queen Medb's invaders. Transformed by rage, roaring like a lion, he killed hundreds – no, thousands – of enemies. He crushed their severed heads to make brain-balls, and built walls with their dead bodies.

Tragic and terrible were his battles against his boyhood friends who were now fighting in Queen Medb's armies. For three days he fought his old comrade Ferdiad [Fear-dee-ah], until death came close to both of them. Ferdiad died, but Cu Chulainn survived, weeping, weak and wounded. Lugh, thegod of the sun, made him whole again, but the war gods refused to give him an outright victory.

Yet again, Queen Medb's and Cu Chulainn's men stood ready to fight when a tremendous bellowing began.

The mountains echoed. The air rang. The ground rumbled.

For safety during this terrible war, the Brown Bull of Ulster was being led out of the kingdom. But the moment it stepped on to Connacht soil, the best bull there roared a challenge. The two magic creatures chased each other all through Ireland, fighting night and day. At last, the Brown Bull won the battle – then collapsed and died.

Queen Medb's war had been in vain.

Queen Medb went home to Connacht, angry, ashamed and disappointed. So many fine men had died for nothing, and she had lost the Brown Bull for ever.

But the fires of pride and anger still smouldered in Medb's heart. She still hated Cu Chulainn, and he was still alive, ready to fight against her.

Already, Medb had been helped by magic in her battles against Cu Chulainn. It came from the ghostly, ghastly Morrigan, the gloating goddess of blood and death. Drawn by the clash of weapons and the cries of dying men, the Morrigan haunted the

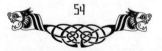

battlefield whenever Medb's men fought against Cu Chulainn.

Like a pitiless crow that feeds on carrion[1] flesh, she could never keep away. Men saw her and shuddered as she changed into the shape of a raven and perched close to where they were fighting. Would she feed on them that nightfall?

Usually, the Morrigan did not take sides. Death was all she cared about. But, in the fight for the great Brown Bull, she had grown, like Medb, to hate Cu Chulainn. Why? Because when she appeared to him as a young woman, he refused to love her, as this would mean embracing his death. Angry and offended, the Morrigan vowed revenge.

As an eel, the Morrigan tripped Cu Chulainn, so he fell. As a she-wolf, she chased cattle to trample him. As a young cow, she nearly gored him right through with her magic horns. Cu Chulainn escaped, injuring her instead, though the struggle left him completely exhausted.

If Cu Chulainn could fight Death herself and win, the hour of his doom was not at hand. So the Morrigan made peace, for the

1. dead.

moment, with CuChulainn. But Medb had other magic brewing.

Cu Chulainn was protected by many enchantments, but every magic spell has a weakness, a way it can be broken, and Medb knew perfectly well how to break his. She called on the six daughters of Calatin, a famous druid, to help her.

The six witches were ugly and miserable and cruel, but also very clever. They sent nightmares and visions to tease and torment Cu Chulainn. How could he survive them? He seemed to be constantly surrounded by fighting men, all begging for his help to save them. He saw champions stepping forward, daring him to fight. He saw his own limbs, hacked and bleeding. He leapt up, grabbed his weapons, rushed towards the fight – but the ghostly sights faded away.

Confused and dismayed by these nightmares, Cu Chulainn went to find his comrades in their camp. By the roadside he met a group of ragged old women, huddled over a fire. An iron cooking-pot seethed and belched beside them. 'Come share our meal, fine young sir!' they cried. 'You'll dine with us today!' Cu Chulainn had no choice. Back

then it was a very serious insult indeed to refuse a stranger's hospitality.

So, cautiously, unwillingly, he sat down by the pot, and the old women gave him meat. He ate. He chewed, He swallowed. It was disgusting! 'We're very poor, so it's just stewed dog,' they said, grinning horribly.

The world went black before Cu Chulainn's eyes. He gasped and retched and shivered. But it was too late! The witches had tricked him. They knew, he knew, Medb knew, and the Morrigan knew: if Cu Chulainn eats dog meat, he will die. Cathbad, the wise Druid, had informed him of this when he gave him his warrior name. Now he, Cu Chulainn – Culann's Hound – had eaten one of his own kind.

'Well, they've still got to kill me!' Cu Chulainn said bravely to himself, as he hurried away from the six witches. 'I'm young, magical, and I've got the best weapons and armour…'

Then he stopped, and in a second his blood turned to water.

Crouched beside a stream, just a few steps away, there was another woman, gleefully washing bright red blood off weapons and

armour. To his horror, Cu Chulainn saw that they were his!

But this was not another witch. No – it was the Morrigan. Death had come to claim him. She got up, looking young and lovely again, and handed him his weapons. 'Fight bravely,' she smiled, 'until we meet again!' And then she vanished.

Medb's army was close by, led by Lugaid [Lewy], Medb's champion. Cu Chulainn rode grimly towards him. His horses wept tears of blood, as they too saw death approaching, but Cu Chulainn urged them bravely onwards. With his mighty arms, he hurled his magic spear – that never missed – towards the champion Lugaid. It sliced through nine men, but flew on and on, passing Lugaid by. It seemed that the magic of Death was now stronger than all.

Lugaid caught the spear and hurled it back. It struck Cu Chulainn right in the stomach, wounding him horribly. But he was still alive, and still dangerous. No-one dared approach him. In agony, he slowly crawled, inch by inch, until his back could rest against a tree. There, staring straight at life and death, Ulster's hero died.

The Morrigan, now in raven shape, flew down and perched on Cu Chulainn's still and lifeless shoulder.

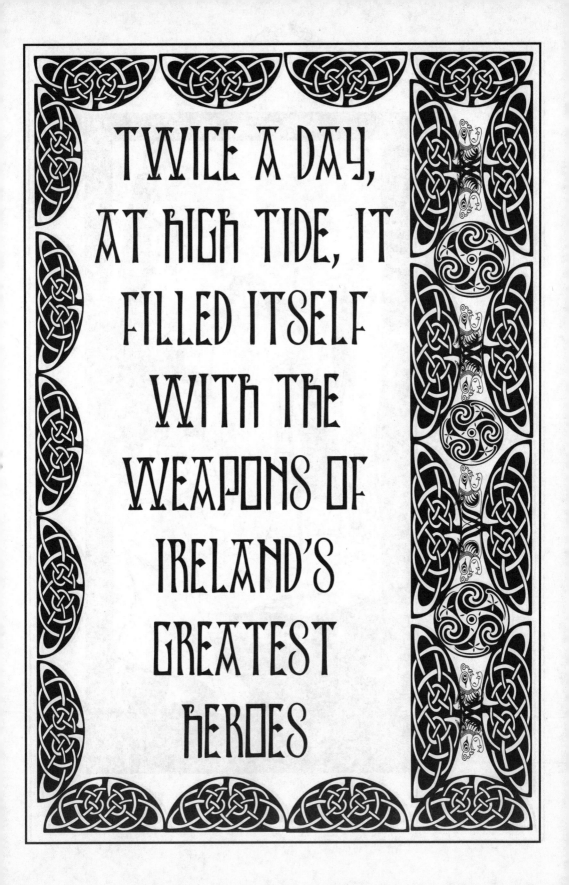

TWICE A DAY,
AT HIGH TIDE, IT
FILLED ITSELF
WITH THE
WEAPONS OF
IRELAND'S
GREATEST
HEROES

CHAPTER 3

The Adventures of Fionn Mac Cumhaill [Finn MacCool]

The gods were not kind to Chief Cumhaill [Cool] of Ireland. He was brave and loyal; they might have wanted to reward him with more. But no, what they gave him was a choice: He could stay single and live long, but leave no son to lead his clan, or he could fall in love and marry – but be killed at his next battle.

Cumhaill was not afraid of danger. All Ireland knew how well he led his warriors – the bold, bloodthirsty Fianna [Fee-ann-a]. They were the Irish High King's finest fighting men, and they had faced fearsome ordeals to join Cumhaill's army.

Too proud and noble to complain, Cumhaill accepted his fate. For years, he spent long, glorious days hunting and fighting and feasting, out of the sight of women. But his heart was lonely, and the ghosts of his ancestors came to haunt him on dark nights.

'Remember, remember!' they whispered, 'It is our life and strength that supports you! You must leave a son to pass it on, or our clan's great name and fame will die!'

Far away, Princess Muirne [Morna] sighed as she gazed out from her tower at the top of a hill. Her father kept her imprisoned there, so that she would not meet a husband. She had inherited magical blood from her mother, who was from the Otherworld.

Muirne's father, both a king and a druid, knew that magic meant danger. He prophesied that Muirne's son would bring death and destruction. Hopelessly and

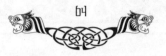

foolishly, defying the gods, he tried to stop this happening.

But Muirne was beautiful and headstrong. One day, she caught sight of Cumhaill, hunting with his hounds, alone. Their eyes met – and they fell in love instantly. Muirne's father, afraid of the dark power that a grandson would bring, would not let them marry – so they ran away together.

They lived wild as outlaws in the woods, with only dogs and wolves and deer for company. They made a house of leafy branches, and a bed of soft moss and wild flowers. A murmuring stream sang them to sleep, and sweet birdsong woke them in the mornings. Free, and delighted to have found love at last, their life was blissful. And, of course, they had a son.

Cumhaill and Muirne were happy, but the Fianna were uneasy. What had love done to their leader? He was shaming and neglecting them! Worst of all, he was failing in his duty to defend Ireland from invaders. Enemies could attack any day!

'Why should Cumhaill still be our chief?', they asked one another, 'when he spends all his time with Muirne?'

Urged on by Goll, the jealous leader of a rival clan, the Fianna fought against Cumhaill. And, as the gods had commanded, Cumhaill was killed in the battle. Goll became leader of the Fianna, and chased Cumhaill's son out of Ireland. Muirne wept bitterly, but she had hope. All was not lost. She was already pregnant, by Cumhaill, and she knew the child would be a boy!

It was so. And, of course, the baby's life was in danger as soon as it was born. Goll wanted to kill him, the last leader of the Cumhaill clan. So, secretly, when the moon was small, Muirne took her boy to the mountains. There, she gave him to two wise women, a witch and a druid.

'Teach him to be a fine warrior,' Muirne said. 'But if you value his life and yours, don't tell anyone about his parents!'

The boy grew tall and good-looking, clever, strong and brave. The women taught him how to hunt and fish and ride and fight. They were as tough as they were wise, and the boy's training was gruelling. To make him run faster, they chased him with sticks from thorn-bushes. They threw him into a pond to force him to learn to swim. But they also

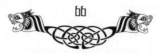

taught him prayers and magic and music and dancing and songs – and how he should, by rights, take the place of his dead father Cumhaill as the glorious leader of the legendary Fianna. After all, his older brother had been chased out of Ireland.

Just once, after six years, his mother came to visit him. He treasured that memory. She drove a magic chariot, decorated with wolf-heads. She sat on his bed, hugged and kissed him. Then she sang him into dreamland with a little sleepy song.

As the boy roamed through the mountain forests, he met other youngsters, riding horses, playing sports and hunting. He became their friend and, soon, their leader. They gave him a nickname, 'Fionn' (bright), and he is still called that to this day.

But Goll heard about the wild boys in the forest, and sent his warriors to catch them. 'Fionn! You must save yourself!' his teachers said. 'It's time to go! Don't try to come back. This is a magical place. You'll never be able to find it again.'

Fionn ran and ran. He tried to find shelter in the houses of chiefs, but they would not hide him for fear of Goll's revenge. Alone and

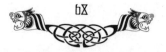

outcast, he had to fight vicious men and savage monsters to survive.

The first man he killed was one of the Fianna who had fought against his father. On the body, Fionn found the magic bag that rightfully belonged to him, as clan leader. It was made from the skin of a beautiful bird that had once been an enchanted woman. Twice a day, at high tide, it filled itself with the weapons of Ireland's greatest heroes.

'Surely, this is a sign from the gods!' Fionn thought. 'I will be chief one day!'

Next, Fionn found himself beside the banks of the beautiful River Boyne. All Ireland's poetry flowed in its swift, bright waters. Telling no-one his name, he found work in the house of Finngeas [Fin-gus], a teacher.

Every day, for seven long years, Finngeas had gone fishing in the river. He wanted to catch the great Salmon of Knowledge – but always his nets were empty. 'If only I could taste that wondrous fish!' he said. 'Then I would understand everything!'

Soon after Fionn arrived at his house, Finngeas was astonished. See there! The great Salmon glowed and glittered in

his net, like a rainbow, like sunrise, like starlight.

Finngeas ordered Fionn to cook the fish and serve it to him for dinner. 'But don't eat it!' he commanded. 'It might kill you!'

Fionn did as he was told, but the Salmon was hot, and burned his thumb when he touched it. To ease the pain, Fionn licked the burn and, by chance, a very tiny piece of the Salmon's skin that had stuck to it.

Fionn's world heaved and reeled. In a dazzling, dizzying flash, he knew! He knew everything, past and present! Only the future still seemed dark – for the moment.

Close by the River Boyne, three goddesses guarded the Well of the Moon. Its water had the power to show what was to happen next, but they would not let anyone drink it. 'No, not unless you give us a golden cup!' they said, chasing Fionn away. But as they flitted around, waving their fin-like hands at him, a drop of magic water from the well of the moon landed on his lips. The universe now held no secrets for Fionn.

It was Samhain[1] [Sav-ahnn], the season of

1. *Celtic festival at the end of October/beginning of November. Modern Halloween (31 October) continues it, mingled with later Christian beliefs.*

the year we call Hallowe'en, when the High King of Ireland called warriors to his court, to hear their complaints against each other. Fionn decided to go there, and demand revenge on Goll for killing Cumhaill, his father.

The High King greeted Fionn, and welcomed him kindly. 'I know you!' he declared. 'You're Cumhaill's son! That was a man I trusted!'

But Samhain is also the time when this world draws closest to the Otherworld. Every Samhain, gods, ghosts and shadows take strange shapes and walk among the living. Every year, for nine years, the High King's palace had been destroyed by an evil Otherworld spirit.

Aillen [Allen] was the spirit's name. He played the harp most beautifully, and sang the most wonderful songs. While his music bound the High King and his warriors by its spell, Aillen would blow great flames of fire from his mouth, burning down the royal palace.

'If any man can kill Aillen', vowed the High King, 'I will give him all that he claims!'

Fionn stepped forward. 'I'm your man!' he said.

But how, Fionn wondered, how could Aillen be killed? He dived deep inside his mind, seeking the magic Salmon's wisdom.

While Fionn was still thinking, a voice boomed out of the crowd.

'I'm Fiacha [Fee-ach-a]!' it said. 'I fought for your father! Take this spear! Its horrible smell will drive Aillen's magic away – so will touching its tip to your forehead!' Fionn gratefully accepted the magical spear.

It was the hour of Aillen's approach. Fionn watched and waited, wide awake, until the spirit's music worked its mischief. As soon as a chance presented itself, he chased Aillen back towards the Otherworld, before the flames could touch the palace. As the dim, dangerous gates of this world gaped wide, Fionn hurled his spear straight through Aillen's heart. He fell to the ground, quite dead. Fionn cut off Aillen's head, stuck it on a tall pole, and carried the grisly trophy back in triumph. The High King was delighted. So were the Fianna. Even Goll, Fionn's enemy, was very impressed indeed.

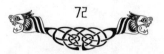

'You've saved my palace!' the king declared, 'and this shall be your reward. I'm making you leader of the Fianna, like your father. My warriors? Chief Goll? Will you follow this young man?' Goll stood proudly and said 'Yes.'

Fionn led the Fianna in many famous battles, and hundreds of stories are told about their strange and daring adventures: how they killed a magic boar and a five-headed giant, fought with gods, and escaped the dreaded death-goddess, Morrigan.

Stories were also told of how they all lived happily in Fionn's great palace, with five druids to guide them, five doctors to heal them, five poets and twelve musicians (including a fairy bard) to cheer their feasts and comfort their sorrows. They had three cup-bearers to serve them, six door-keepers to guard their gates, and servants, huntsmen, horn-blowers, cooks, sewing-women and many more – far too many to mention.

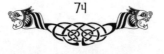

One of the strangest tales tells how Fionn found his marvellous hunting dogs, Bran [Brahn] and Sceolan [Skyo-lin].

Muirne, Fionn's mother, had become a great queen. She decided to visit Fionn. Her sister, Tuiren [Toor-en], a pretty and friendly girl, travelled with her for company.

Almost as soon as they arrived, Iollen [Yoll-an], a brave and famous warrior, fell in love with Tuiren, and soon wanted to marry her. He asked Fionn's permission to get married.

'Yes,' Fionn replied, cautiously. 'But if ever I ask you to send Tuiren back, you must do so straight away.' Puzzled but obedient, Iollen agreed.

Iollen soon married Tuiren, and they were very happy. That is, until Iollen's past lover heard of the wedding, and became furious.

Iollen's ex-lover was no ordinary girl. She belonged to the Otherworld. Quickly, she disguised herself as one of Fionn's servants, and hurried to Iollen's lodgings. 'Greetings from Fionn,' she curtsied low. 'He asks for Tuiren. You must send her.'

Still puzzled, still obedient, Iollen waved goodbye as Tuiren rode off with the 'servant'.

But then Iollen's ex-lover called upon her magic powers – and Tuiren was transformed. She became an Irish hunting dog, swift, lithe, fearless. The 'servant' left her with oneof Fionn's old friends, Fergus MacRoy [Feargus Mack-roy], the Dog-Hater.

But even Fergus could not hate this dog. It was beautiful, gentle and true. But it could not speak, or ask for help. Was Tuiren trapped, for ever?

The next day, Fionn summoned Iollen and said, 'You must bring your bride to visit!' 'But I can't, my lord!' Iollen stammered in reply. 'She set off yesterday to see you – and she's disappeared!'

Fionn was furious. 'I trusted her to your care!' he yelled. 'Unless you bring her to me, unharmed, you will pay for this with your life!'

Iollen searched high and low, but he could not find Tuiren. Not knowing where to turn or who to ask, he went to the Otherworld gate where he used to meet his ex-lover.

Iollen's ex-lover was there, smiling so sweetly and cruelly, as only spirits can do.

'Yes, I'll find Tuiren for you', she said. 'If you'll come back to me, for ever.'

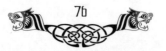

Shocked and ashamed, Iollan agreed – and was dragged down into the Otherworld. Iollen's lover kept her promise: Tuiren changed back into human shape, and returned to Fionn's court – with two puppies.

'These are my children,' Tuiren said. 'They are dogs and they are humans.'

'They will be my companions as long as they live!' said Fionn. He named them Bran and Sceolan.

Fionn was true to his word. The dogs were always with him. They were even there on

that amazing day when Fionn met his wife, the deer-woman.

It was late, and Fionn and the dogs were heading home after hunting in the forest. All of a sudden, a graceful young deer leaped across the path in front of them. But instead of chasing her away, the dogs ran up to her and licked her. And, instead of running off in fright, the deer followed Fionn back home to his palace.

Much later, near midnight, Fionn sat alone. The room was dark, except for firelight, flickering. A slim and delicate young woman, with large, lovely brown eyes, appeared, smiling, in front of him.

'I am the deer who followed you today,' she said gently. 'My name is Sava. I am glad you did not kill me.'

'Once I was human, like you. But I refused to wed an evil druid, so he changed me into a wild deer and drove me into the forest. For three long years, I lived in fear of being chased and killed by huntsmen. But your dogs, which I can see are humans too, recognised me and saved me.'

They married, and Fionn loved her so much that for a long time he stopped hunting

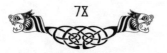

and fighting. But then war came, and Fionn had to leave home to lead the Fianna army.

One day, while Fionn and his men were away, Sava thought she saw Fionn approaching, so she ran out to greet him, full of joy. But all of a sudden Fionn vanished, and as clouds rolled and thundered all around, the evil druid appeared. Beside him, Sava, a young deer again, stood weeping and trembling. Heartbroken, Fionn searched for seven years, but never found Sava. However, one day Bran and Sceolan saved the life of a young boy on the mountainside. Fionn looked at him closely. Yes, the likeness was so strong! This must be Sava's child – and he must be its father!

Fionn named his son Ossian, which means 'Little Deer'. Then, after many years had passed, he chose a new wife, a princess called Grainne [Graw-nyah].
But by now, Fionn was old and grey, and Grainne was young and beautiful. At their wedding feast, she fell in love with a handsome young warrior, Diarmaid [Dermot].

Diarmaid fought in the Fianna. He was loyal to Fionn, but Grainne enchanted him.

They ran away together, and Fionn chased them for sixteen years, all over Ireland. Diarmaid and Grainne escaped, helped by Aengus [Angus], the God of Love, and, persuaded by Aengus, Finn at last agreed to make peace.

But then Fionn played a deadly trick. He challenged Diarmaid to fight a savage boar, although druids had warned that this would kill Diarmaid. As the brave, doomed, Diarmaid lay dying, Fionn refused to fetch him life-saving water. It was the worst thing he ever did, and shameful for a great hero.

Many tales are told about Fionn's ultimate fate. Some say he drowned when he broke a magic spell, and became mortal, like other humans. Some say he became a tall stone pillar, buried deep below a holy building. But others say that Fionn still lives, fast asleep, and will wake when Ireland needs him.

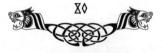

IN ALL OF
BRAN'S
KINGDOM, THERE
WAS NOT A
HOUSE BIG
ENOUGH TO
HOLD HIM.

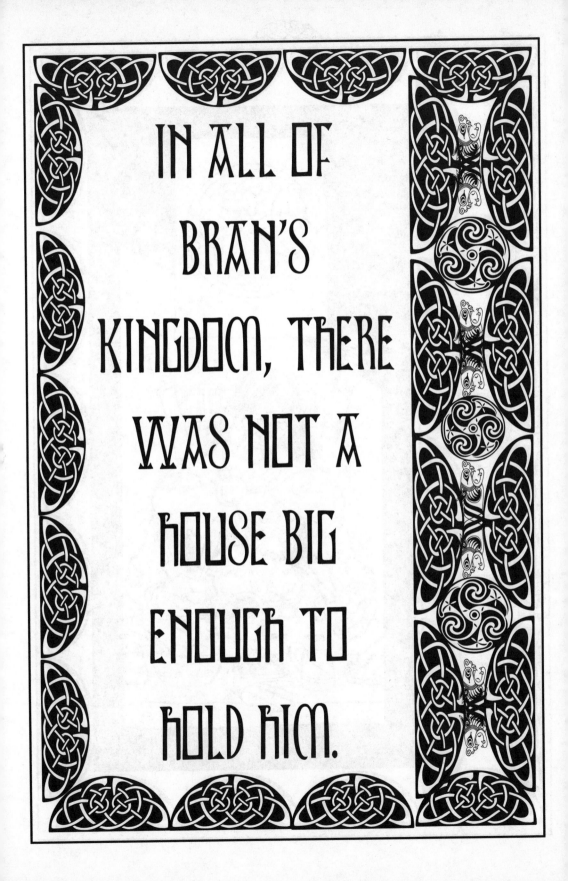

CHAPTER 4

Bran and Branwen

reat-hearted Bran, King of Wales, was as big as a giant. He towered over his people like the tall Welsh mountains, and guarded them like a high stone wall. His head was like a huge, strong rock, his nose like a jutting cliff, and his eyes like pools of water. His hair was black and glossy, like

the feathers of a fierce bird, which is why his father had named him Bran, meaning 'raven'.

In all of Bran's kingdom, there was not a house big enough to hold him. He slept outdoors, like the gods of his country – in caves, under trees, or beneath the stars.

Bran's sister Branwen was the size of a human, but her beauty made her like a goddess. Her hair was as dark as midnight and as shiny as stars; her skin was smooth and delicate, like snow. She was graceful, like young trees in the forest, and her smile was as bright and radiant as sunrise.

Branwen had a fine character, as well. She was wise and loyal, clever and hard-working, loving, generous and kind.

At the time this story begins, Branwen was not married. Instead, she lived with Bran at Harlech in north Wales. Bran's three strong, handsome brothers shared their royal court. Their names were Manawyddan, Nissyen and Evnissyen [Mann-ou-with-ann, Niss-ee-an and Ev-niss-ee-an].

One day, Bran was sitting on a high rock, looking out to sea. His three brothers were with him. Many other Welsh nobles

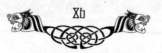

were there as well, all patiently waiting to obey Bran's orders.

'What's that I see?' cried Bran, using the excellent sight awarded him by his huge eyes. 'It's – let me count! – eleven, twelve, thirteen sailing ships, all heading this way!'

'You there!', Bran commanded one of his servants. 'Run as fast as you can, and find out who they are!'

'And you!' Bran yelled to another, 'Tell the soldiers to get ready! Those ships might be invaders!'

But the ships carried the welcome sign of peace – a shield turned upside-down. All on board seemed friendly – and what fine visitors they were! Their ships were streamlined and seaworthy, expertly made of strong timber. The men were handsome and courteous, and dressed in rich golden robes. Their horses were magnificent, too – sleek and swift as the wind.

'We come from Ireland, in peace,' they said. 'Our leader is the Irish High King. His name is Mallolwch [Mah-hloll-ooch], and he has travelled all this way because he wants to marry Branwen!' Proud King Mallolwch stepped ashore, smiling graciously. 'I have

heard of your sister's great beauty,' he said. 'Surely a royal wedding – with me! – would bring peace and friendship between our nations.'

'That's a grand hope! Peace! What a good idea!' Bran agreed. 'Now come on, let's feast together!'

The Welsh and their welcome Irish guests ate and drank far, far into the night. They sat in a massive tent, just big enough for Bran to squeeze into. King Mallolwch was given the chair of honour, between Bran and Branwen. He seemed delighted that this good and lovely woman was soon to be his bride. Branwen seemed happy, too, though at the time no-one had consulted her feelings.

But one man was not happy at the feast, or in the days that followed. Evnissyen, Bran's brother, was furious that no-one had asked him to give his permission for his sister Branwen's wedding. By law and tradition, they did not need to; Bran made all the big decisions. But Evnissyen was jealous, and wanted to share Bran's power.

So, evilly, cruelly, Evnissyen attacked the Irish visitors' wonderful horses. Words cannot describe the terrible things he did.

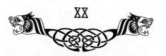

When the Irish king heard of this appalling act, his heart swelled with rage and hatred. 'I must leave this bloody, backward, barbaric country!' he said, and headed for his ships.

When servants came to Bran with the news that King Mallolwch was leaving, he was extremely worried. And when he heard about Evnissyen's terrible crime, he was just as angry as the Irish. The attack on the Irish horses was an insult to his guests, to Branwen, and to Wales! It broke one of the great laws of the Celtic lands – hospitality to strangers. But now the dreadful deed was done, he could not undo the damage. All he could do, to help his country, was to try to persuade the Irish not to declare war.

Straight away, he sent urgent messengers to the Irish king. 'Bran begs you not to go!' they pleaded. 'He wants to offer you rich gifts, as a sign of friendship. He'll give you his best horses to replace the ones that Evnissyen killed and injured. And he'll give you a stick of pure silver, as tall as he is, and as thick as his huge fingers – plus a solid gold plate as broad as his own enormous face.'

'Bran also wants you to know that, if he could, he'd kill Evnissyen for attacking

your horses. But our laws forbid brothers killing brothers, as I'm sure you'll understand.'

'That's well said!' replied King Mallolwch. 'I'll call my men to a Grand Council, and ask them to stay.'

Because of Bran's generous offer, the Irish visitors agreed to remain in Wales. But, as Bran sat talking to King Mallolwch the next day, he thought that the king seemed sullen and depressed.

'Does the attack on your horses still sadden and shame you?' Bran asked. 'Well, I'm not really surprised! But I'll give you such a fine gift that all thoughts of the insult will vanish from your mind!'

'I'll give you the gift of my magic cauldron. Any man who's killed only has to sit inside it, and he'll be reborn, good as new! There's just one slight problem,' he admitted. 'He won't be able to speak – though I think he'll be able to hear.'

Bran was as good as his word. The next day, he handed over his cauldron.

King Mallolwch was delighted. 'Thank you!' He beamed. 'But tell me! Where did you get such a splendid treasure?'

'Well, strangely enough, from Ireland!' Bran replied. 'I got the cauldron from a man who lived there once. I think he must have brought it with him.'

'Ah-ha!' said King Mallolwch. 'I think I know that cauldron! One day, out hunting in Ireland, I rode past a deep, dark lake. A rough-looking, ragged, red-haired man was staggering out of it, dragging the cauldron behind him. He must have found it there.'

'Maybe it comes from the Otherworld, or perhaps it belonged to a god! Everyone knows that they live in lakes and rivers – and that there are ways into the Otherworld through water.'

'He was a wild creature,' continued Mallolwch, 'and so was his wife! She was twice as big and noisy and dirty as him. I let them stay at my palace for a year, but they grew so rude and rowdy that I decided to get rid of them. I built them an iron house, locked them in, then lit a huge fire all around it. When the house glowed white-hot, they roared out through the melting walls and ran away from Ireland.'

'Yes, they came here,' said Bran, 'So far, they've not caused any trouble. I usually keep

them busy defending the frontiers.' The two kings sealed the bargain by organising an excellent feast. The next day Branwen left with Mallolwch, to start her new life in Ireland.

The Irish people were pleased to welcome Branwen as their queen. When, within a year, she had a baby son, almost everyone was delighted. However, a few Irish chiefs still could not forget how King Mallolwch and his horses had been insulted and attacked in Wales. They muttered bad things about the Welsh, especially Branwen.

King Mallolwch heard these whispers, and over time he began to take heed of them. He threw Branwen out of his royal chambers, and sent her to work in the palace kitchens. Some people even said that he hit her – even though she was his wife and his queen. Branwen spent three years slaving over heavy, dirty tasks. She swept and cleaned, washed greasy dishes, and spent hours kneading dough to make bread. Every day, the castle butcher beat her, his hands all foul and smelly with scraps of raw meat and fresh animal blood.

Why did nobody rescue her? The Irish didn't help because they were so scared of King Mallolwch. And because the king had stopped all ships sailing between Wales and Ireland, King Bran and his people could not find out what was happening.

But Branwen was clever, and found a way to tell her brother Bran how badly the Irish were treating her. Gently, patiently, she tamed a starling that came searching for scraps of food. The wise women of Wales were famous for their ability to talk to birds, so she wrote an urgent message on a tiny piece of parchment, tied it to the starling's leg, and told it to fly straight to Bran.

As soon as Bran received Branwen's message, his blood boiled with anger. 'Come on, men!' he bellowed. 'We're going to attack!' All the lords of Bran's council agreed to go with him. They left just seven young noblemen to guard and govern Wales.

Bran led his army to Ireland. His men sailed in ships, but there was no ship big enough to hold Bran, so he waded across the sea. He carried his favourite musicians on his broad shoulders.

One day, King Mallolwch's servants were herding pigs by the shore. Out to sea, they saw something strange – very strange – approaching. They immediately ran to inform the king. 'Sire!' they panted, out of breath, 'There's a forest on the water! It's moving right towards us, and fast too!'

King Mallolwch was startled. 'Go on! Tell me more!' he said. 'We also saw a tall mountain, moving!' the servants cried. Fearfully, they added, 'There's a huge cliff near its peak, and two pools of water.'

Branwen smiled as the news spread through the palace. She knew what that mountain was! It was Bran, her giant brother! The cliff must be his nose, the pools his eyes, and the forest his ships' masts. They were coming to rescue her!

The Irish lords were frightened. 'We can't fight a giant!' they all agreed. 'Let's all head inland, across that deep river. If we destroy the bridge once we've all got across, the Welsh won't be able to reach us!'

But how wrong they were! When Bran saw the broken bridge, he found a simple way to replace it. He lay down and stretched out like a bridge himself – and his

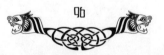

men walked over him to the other side of the river.

King Mallolwch had no choice. Now it was his turn to welcome visitors. He sent his messengers to Bran. 'Come this way, my lord,' they fawned and smiled. 'The High King greets you!'

Mallolwch did not want to fight. So how could he calm Bran's anger? There was just one way – to give up the kingship, and make Branwen's young son king.

So that was what he did, or rather, promised. But it wasn't enough. Bran was still furious about Mallolwch's cruel, shameful treatment of Branwen.

'We know!' the Irish lords said, at last. 'You must build Bran a house, as fine as you can. He's never had a palace before. It will be a great honour!'

Branwen stepped forward. 'Brother, please agree to this,' she begged. 'I don't want a war fought because of me. It will only harm innocent people.'

Bran agreed with Branwen's wise advice, so the house was built – huge, strong and splendid. There was room for Bran and all his army inside. But Mallolwch's men had played

a trick. Inside Bran's share of the house they had left a hundred sacks. They told Bran that the sacks were full of flour, but each contained a fierce Irish warrior.

Evnissyen had come to Ireland with Bran. He eyed the sacks suspiciously, then squeezed each one extremely hard, until the warrior inside was dead. Mallolwch was none the wiser.

That night, Mallolwch held a great feast for Bran and the Welsh and Irish armies. He announced that Branwen's son would be the next king, and bring peace between Wales and Ireland.

Bran and Branwen glowed with pleasure, but, once again, their brother Evnissyen was jealous. He picked up Branwen's son by the heels and threw him into the fire!

Branwen screamed, and tried to rescue her boy. But the flames were too fierce and deadly. Bran pulled her back, saving her life. But seeing the blazing Irish eyes that had just seen their heir thrown into the fire, he grabbed his sword and shield.

The battle that followed was savage and bloody. Such fighting had never been seen in Ireland. The Welsh looked liked winning,

until Mallolwch's men fought their way towards the fire, carrying the magic cauldron. They gathered up the Irish dead and threw them inside the cauldron. Then, just as Bran had promised, the dead men were reborn, and straight away started fighting again.

Evnissyen watched, and his cruel, jealous heart trembled with a new passion. 'I can't let all the Welsh soldiers be killed,' he said. 'I must help my country!'

So Evnissyen hid among the dead Irish, and was thrown into the cauldron with them. But instead of jumping out alive, he stretched himself out – like Bran at the bridge – and completely shattered the cauldron! The magic of the cauldron destroyed Evnissyen, who broke into pieces too, but he died proud and happy. At last, he had done something to bring peace instead of killing all the time.

Without the magic cauldron, the Irish soon ran out of soldiers. The Welsh won the battle – though they had only seven men left alive. Bran survived as well, of course, but he had been wounded in the foot by a spear tipped with poison.

'When I die, you must cut off my head,' he commanded the men, 'and carry it to London.

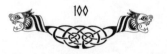

There you must bury it, facing France.' He smiled, 'You will have a very long journey!'

'First, you must feast at my old royal court, then go to Pembroke, in south Wales. But remember! Keep all doors facing south completely closed! If you open them, my head will rot away.'

Mournfully, the Welshmen did as Bran commanded, and took Branwen home with them. As they landed in Wales, she looked back to Ireland, where her son lay dead and buried. Her husband, King Mallolwch, was dead too, killed in the terrible battle.

'I should never have been born,' Branwen sighed. 'My beauty has caused so much suffering! The men of two fine countries have been slaughtered because of me.'

She wept, and as her heart broke with sorrow she joined her husband and son in death. Bran's men buried her where she died.

As for Bran – well, he died too, from the spear's poison. But his head went on living. The Welshmen carried it with them, and their journey was full of wonders.

At the royal court near Harlech, three magic birds sang so sweetly that the men stayed for seven years. The birds came from

Rhiannon [Hree-ann-on], goddess-queen. 'They can wake the dead from their slumbers,' she smiled, 'and send blissful sleep to the living.' At Pembroke, the Welshmen forgot all their sadness and suffering. It was as if Bran lived, and was still with them, their leader and companion.

They spent eighty years of pleasure and joy at Pembroke, blissfully ignorant of what had happened. Then, one day, forgetting what Bran had said, the Welshmen opened a door facing southwards. Suddenly all the pain from their wounds and their bitter memories rushed back – and they remembered that Bran, their noble leader, had died.

Sadly, they hurried on towards London. Each day, Bran's head seemed smaller and weaker. Just in time, they reached London's White Hill by the River, and lovingly buried Bran's head there.

Then they turned and began to walk westwards to Wales, their minds full of sad thoughts and memories. But suddenly, their pain and sorrow disappeared. Yes! Surely, yes! They knew that sound! They heard Bran's voice calling!

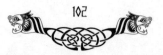

'While my head stays safely buried here', it boomed, 'all will be well with this island. No plagues will come from across the sea. My people will find happiness!'

CHAPTER 5

Lludd and Llevelys

King Beli of Britain had four sons: Lludd, Casswallawn, Nynnyaw and Llevelys [Hleeth, Cass-wah-hlawn, Nyn-yow and Hlev-ell-ees]. They were all very fine fellows, but this story is about just two of them.

Lludd, the eldest, ruled Britain after his father died. He

was a strong king and a brave fighter. He built stone walls around London, his favourite city, and constructed many splendid palaces. You could see their tall towers, with bright flags fluttering in the breeze, from many miles away.

Lludd was friendly and generous – good things for a king to be. He helped the poor, protected the weak, and loved feasting. The country and its people grew rich during his reign – that is, until the trouble started.

But before you read on, you should know that King Lludd's best friend in the world was Llevelys, his youngest brother.

Llevelys had married a French princess, and was the King of France, across the sea. Although he lived so far away, he still loved hearing stories about Britain.

Then, one day, the stories stopped. Weeks passed, then years, and still Llevelys received no news. No panting couriers arrived on horseback, no dusty messengers on foot. Not even the odd magic bird carrying secret letters over the water.

Without exactly knowing why, Levelys felt very worried.

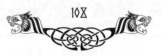

Three Terrible Plagues

It turned out that here were very good reasons for Lludd's long silence. Three plagues were devastating Britain!

The first plague was an invasion of elves – the Korriganed [Korr-ee-gan-ay][1], or 'Little People'. Their senses were so keen and sharp that they could hear every word that was spoken. No-one could keep secrets anymore – not lovers or children or spies. Everything anyone said was heard, remembered and repeated. Even Lludd himself, with all his power, could not stop the elves eavesdropping. It was scary, spooky and quite maddening!

The second plague was a frightful scream that rang through every house each May Eve.[2] It was such a loud, wild, savage sound that people died from the shock of hearing it. No-one knew who or what made the noise, or why, or where it came from. No-one could chase it, catch it, hush it or stop it. It was absolutely terrifying!

1. *A Celtic word for elves or fairies, still used in Brittany.*
2. *The night before 1 May (Beltane), the Celtic festival celebrating the start of summer, and the sun.*

The third and last plague was puzzling, and, for King Lludd, very, very expensive. No matter how much food his servants prepared each night, it was all gone the next morning. Whole barns full of grain, big ponds full of fish, heaped baskets of eggs, heavy barrels of wine, and plump herds of cattle all just completely vanished overnight!

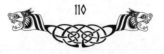

Lludd Seeks Advice

King Lludd tried as hard as he could to end the plagues, but nothing would stop them. So he called a grand council of his warrior lords, and asked them to advise him. 'Go and see your brother Llevelys, King of France,' they said. 'He is wise, and skilled in magic!'

Secretly, and in silence, Lludd set sail for France. He left in the middle of a dark, gloomy night, so that no-one would know he was going. He felt deeply ashamed that he could not help his people. And, of course, he did not want the elves to find out any more about his plans.

He sailed on, and was very surprised to see another royal ship approaching. Imagine his delight when he got close enough to see that it carried Llevelys, his brother!

'Welcome! Welcome!' Llevelys said. 'I had a feeling you might be coming. So I sailed out to meet you – but, Lludd, my dear man, why are you looking so glum and grim and sorrowful?'

'I can't tell you here on the open deck', King Lludd whispered. 'THEY will be listening! But we need to talk! It's a

matter of life and death! How can we be private?'

Llevelys thought hard, then sent for the very best metal workers in his kingdom. He told them to make a long, curved trumpet of bronze, with a wide bell-mouth at each end.

Quickly, they hammered and soldered and polished; in a few days, the trumpet was ready. 'If we speak into this,' Llevelys explained, 'our words will stay safe inside it. The winds won't blow them back to Britain, and the evil elves won't hear them!'

'We must take it in turns to speak and listen,' he continued, holding the trumpet up to his mouth. 'Look! Like this! It's easy!'

Yes, it was easy, but it didn't work! What a disappointment! Every word the brothers spoke came out tangled and twisted and broken. 'This wretched thing's no use!' Lludd complained crossly. 'I can't understand you!'

Llevelys thought again. 'Ah! Now I see!' he said. 'A devil is haunting our trumpet!' We should wash it out with the finest French wine. That should get rid of the problem!'

So they did, and the devil staggered away, all squelchy and soggy and smelly. After that, the shiny speaking-trumpet worked well. Every word came through perfectly.

'I need your help, brother!' King Lludd said. 'Can you try some magic?'

A Magic Mixture

Llevelys laughed. 'What else?' he said. 'Now, go ahead. Tell me!'

'You have three problems,' Llevelys said at last. 'So, here are three solutions. Follow my instructions, step by step, and Britain will be plague-free!'

'First take these flies and let them breed lots more. Then kill them all, keeping just a few alive in case you need them in future.'

'Dry the dead insects, crush them up, then mix the powder with water. You must guard this mixture with your life, and carry it home to Britain.'

'Next, call a meeting of your people. Invite all the elves to come, too. Say you need their help to end the plague, but sprinkle the mixture over them! You'll find that it doesn't harm your people at all, but for the elves, it's deadly! If it doesn't get rid of them in a week – well, then I'm not a king or a magician!'

Lludd did what Llevelys told him, and the first plague ended. All words were safe once more, and all could speak freely.

'Good!' said Llevelys, when he heard the news. 'Now, for your second plague problem,

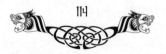

it seems that we must stop the dragons causing those fearsome, fatal noises!'

Lludd was dumbfounded. 'Dragons! What dragons? Where? How? Why?' he gasped, astonished.

'Don't interrupt!' said Llevelys. 'Two monstrous dragons are fighting in the skies above your kingdom. You must find the exact centre of your land and dig a huge pit there, to trap them.'

'Fill the pit with sweet, sticky mead – you'll need a lot! – and spread a silk sheet over it. Find a place close by to hide, and you'll see dragons approaching.'

'At first, they'll look like big lumbering beasts, but suddenly they'll soar into the sky. Their true and terrible shape will be revealed, and they'll fight until they're exhausted. Next, they'll change into pigs, drop down into the pit, drink the mead, and fall asleep snoring.'

'Tie the silk sheet round the sleeping pigs, as tight as you can, and carry them to your strongest mountain fortress. Bury them deep under the ground, and pile huge rocks on top of them. If they stay safely shut away, you'll have no more dragons in the land of Britain!'

Lludd caught the dragons, and the second plague ended. The peace and quiet that followed felt wonderful.

'How do you know what to do?' Lludd exclaimed. 'Who taught you all this magic?'

'Never mind that now,' Llevelys said. 'We must solve your final problem!'

Greedy Giant

'I can tell that a mighty, greedy giant is bewitching all your servants. He casts a spell that makes them fall asleep in the middle of their duties. They stay like statues all night long, and don't see him stomping through your palace, munching food and grabbing and snatching.'

'You must watch for him yourself one night, and stay awake and challenge him. I think a tub of icy water should help. Just jump inside it if you're drowsy!'

'The giant is stupid – as most giants are – but he's absolutely massive. Just one flick of his finger could break your neck. Be very, very careful!'

Lludd was strong and brave, and knew his duty as king, so he sat shivering, and waited. Then the ground shook, the moon and stars were blotted out, and the biggest giant he had ever seen strode into the palace.

The giant filled his basket with enough food for a hundred men, but was still hungry for more. Disappointed, he lumbered off into the night. Lludd got up and raced after him.

'Stop, giant! Stop, thief!' he shouted, furiously. 'You're making my people hungry! I'm going to fight and kill you! Put down that basket, and prepare to die!'

Lludd battled the giant for hours and hours, their swords flashing and sparking in fury. They both fought well and bravely, but neither seemed to be winning.

At last, Lludd made the giant trip over and fall – Crash! Smash! Thump! – with a roar and rumble like thunder. Too huge and too heavy, he couldn't get up. The giant begged Lludd for mercy.

'I'll give back all I took,' he whimpered, 'I'll never steal again! Let me live! Please, please, please let me live, and I'll be your servant for ever!'

'Get up!' said Lludd, wiping the blood off his sword. 'Go away! And stop that snivelling!'

'I've ended three plagues, with my brother's help. That's enough excitement! I'd like a quiet life from now on, without too much magic!'

The rest of Lludd's reign was peaceful, and brought great happiness to Britain.

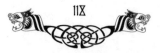

LIKE FLOWERS
THAT FADE
AFTER THEY ARE
PICKED,
BLODEUWEDD'S
SWEET NATURE
WITHERED

CHAPTER 6

True Love, Tragic Love

Etain the Beautiful

Gods and kings loved her. yet none could keep her. Etain [Ee-taw-in] was the loveliest, most beautiful woman in the world – and the most longed-for.

Poets praised Etain's hair ('Gold, like the sun!'), her lips ('As red as rowan berries!'), and her eyes ('Like raindrops on

flowers!'). Etain's glorious looks and power to win men's hearts came from Tir nan Og, the Otherworld. She had been blessed by Danu, the great goddess who brought life – and death – to people in Celtic lands.

King Midhir [Mee-dheer] of the Otherworld heard of Etain's beauty and sent Aengus, god of love, to fetch her. But before Etain's father would let her go, Aengus had to work for him. Helped by magic, and his secret love for Etain, Aengus completed all the tasks, and brought Etain safely to Midhir.

Proudly, Midhir welcomed Etain to his palace, built inside an enchanted mountain. However, he had neglected to mention that he already had a wife. Her name? Fierce Queen Fuamnach [Foo-um-nach].

Angry and jealous, Fuamnach cast a spell. She turned Etain into water, then a worm, then finally a butterfly. But Etain – glowing, shimmering, humming, now a magical creature – would not leave Midhir's side, and was still extraordinarily beautiful.

Fuamnach was furious and called wild winds to blow Etain far out to sea. For seven long years, Etain the butterfly fluttered and struggled. At last, finding herself ashore, she

landed on a cloak worn by Aengus – the young god, the first to love her. His magic turned her into a woman every night, though by day she was still a butterfly. For centuries they lived and loved like this – until Fuamnach found them!

Fuamnach still hated Etain. Again, she sent wicked winds to plague her. For seven more years, Etain was blown around and battered by storms until her demise seemed certain. But somehow she reached land and sought shelter in a fine royal palace. Here was music and feasting, a good fire, and good company!

Exhausted, Etain fluttered down towards the king and his guests at table. She landed in a glass of wine – and was straight away swallowed by the queen!

But Etain did not perish inside the queen. The queen gave birth to the most beautiful baby daughter, and Etain was reborn as a human. She grew up gracious, kind, and married Eochaid [Yoch-hee], the High King of Ireland. He was a good man, and Etain loved him. But he had a brother…

Eochaid's brother – Ailill [All-yill] – made himself very ill with his love for Etain. To

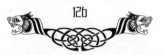

save his life, Etain agreed, unhappily, to spend a night with him. But when she arrived at the meeting place, Ailill was not there.

Instead, she found Midhir, whom she had loved long ago. He was still tall and strong and handsome. But, now human, Etain had no memory of their past life in the Otherworld. 'Surely you know who I am!' Midhir cried. 'See! I'm a king and a god! I made Ailill sick just so I could see you again!'

Etain ran back home trembling, her mind in a whirl. She was met with startling news. Ailill had recovered from his sickness!

Twice more Etain met Midhir, though no-one else could see or hear him. Slowly, she began to remember her past. But who was she, goddess or human?

Soon after, High King Eochaid was out hunting when Midhir appeared beside him. One challenged the other to a game of chess. Three games they played together; each time, the stakes were higher.

Eochaid won the first two games; his prizes were land and horses. Midhir won the third game. His prize? More than anything, he wanted Etain!

Eochaid refused, but offered instead just a small kiss from Etain. 'Just one!' he growled. 'And that's too many! But fair's fair, you've won. Be here in a month – your prize will await you!'

The dreadful day came. Eochaid and his soldiers picked up their weapons, put on their armour, and waited for Midhir. Yes, they'd let him kiss Etain for his prize, but after that, they'd kill him! Midhir rode up, proud and splendid. He seized Etain, kissing her passionately. Then he turned them both into swans. They soared high, high, high into the air, and flew away – forever.

Some say that Etain and Midhir went to the Otherworld, where they may still be living today. They say Aengus still loves Etain, too, and hopes, some time, to win her back. Others say that Midhir agreed to hand Etain back, but then played a trick on Eochaid. He showed him fifty identical women, most of whom were magic spirits. Midhir asked Eochaid which one was Etain. Eochaid chose the wrong woman. Instead he picked Etain's daughter, who looked very much like her! But although Ecohaid loved her like a father, he never found his Etain.

Deirdre of the Sorrows

From the very beginning, Deirdre [Dear-dree] was doomed. Doomed to suffer – and bring suffering to everyone who loved her.

Deirdre's father was a famous bard, Fedlimid [Fail-im-ee]. Before Deirdre was born, Fedlimid hosted a feast for the Irish king and many warrior heroes. As Felimid's pregnant wife served drinks, her unborn baby cried out aloud. It was a blood-curdling shriek that frightened all who heard it.

Druids at the feast foretold the baby's tragic future. It would be a girl, to be called Deirdre, with blonde hair like primroses, green eyes like grass, and pink cheeks like foxgloves. Men would think her beautiful – and that would lead to disaster. Three of Ulster's finest men would die because of her, the druids said.

The king of Ulster, Conchobar MacNessa [Conn-or Mack Ness-ah] was a guest at Fedlimid's feast. After hearing the prophecy, he worried that Deirdre's foretold beauty would cause bickering amongst his men, so he decided to do something about it.

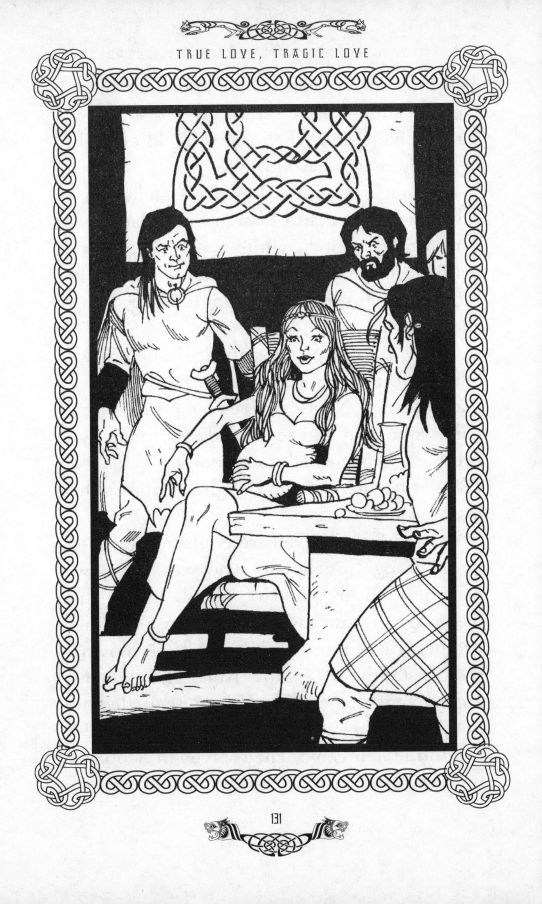

The king gave orders that, upon her birth, Deirdre should be raised in the forest, out of sight of men, and when she was old enough, he would marry her himself.

One day, in winter, Deirdre watched as a raven ate the remains of a calf that had died. The bright blood, white snow and dark feathers fascinated her. 'If there is a man in those powerful colours, I want to marry him!' she said.

Deirdre's old nurse sighed. 'I should not tell you this,' she said, 'but there is such a man. Young Naoise [Nee-shee] has black hair, white skin and red blood. So do his two brothers – they're all good-looking.' Deirdre clapped her hands with delight. 'Naoise's the man for me!'

And so it was. Deirdre could not bear to marry King Conchobar, who was, by now, very old and grey and wrinkled. Before the wedding, she ran away with Naoise and his brothers! At first, they hid in Ulster, moving on constantly to escape King Conchobar's angry, vengeful soldiers. Then they fled to Scotland, living as hideaways in the wild and beautiful Glen Etive. They stayed in Scotland for years, poor, cold, hungry – but happy.

Then King Conchobar sent ambassadors, including the brave hero, Fergus MacRoy, to ask them to come home again. Ulster needed great fighters like Naoise and his brothers.

But King Conchobar was not playing fair. Yes, he needed warriors, but he wanted the lovely Deirdre much more. However, Deirdre did not know this, so she agreed that it was their duty to go back to Ulster.

As they neared King Conchobar's palace, Deirdre had terrible nightmares, full of death and destruction. She saw birds dropping blood from the sky, and Naoise wearing a blood-red crown. Then, the moment they arrived, Deirdre was seized and bound in chains. Servants dragged her away by her hair. King Conchobar grinned, gloating.

At the same time, warriors loyal to the king attacked Naoise and his brothers. Fergus MacRoy heard their cries, and rushed to defend them. He had not brought them back to Ulster for this fate! But his help came too late. Naoise was dead.

King Conchobar married Deirdre, but she brought him no happiness. She refused to look at him, or even speak to him. Furious at

her constant disdain for him, Conchobar arranged to send her to Naoise's killers, to be their slave.

Deirdre said nothing, as usual, but she escaped King Conchobar and his killers! She hurled herself from the chariot taking her to slavery. It was one year and a day after Naoise was killed.

A huge tree grew from the spot where Deirdre chose to die. Its branches climbed towards heaven. And they twined so closely with the tree above Naoise's nearby grave that the two have never, ever, been untangled.

Houarn and Bellah

They called it the lake of death. It was deep and dark, gloomy and menacing. Many brave men made the journey there, but they were never seen again.

The last man to visit the lake was young Houarn [Hoo-ahn], from Brittany. This is his story.

Houarn and Bellah [Bell-ah] had been best friends all their lives. Now they wanted to get married. But their parents were dead, and they were very poor. They could not afford a cottage, and had no money to raise a cow, a pig, or even a few chickens.

'I must find a job!' said Houarn, at last. 'I'm going to the town.'

'Take care, my love!' Bellah replied. 'And carry these lucky charms with you! Look, here's a little bell, and a knife. My mother gave them to me. She gave me this stick, as well. But I'll keep that, in case I need it.'

In town, Houarn met many poor people like himself, all trying, but failing, to make money. He also heard rumours of a mysterious lake, full of hidden treasures. Houarn went to the lake, and climbed on

board a boat shaped like a sleeping swan. Then all of a sudden the swan woke up, spread its wings – and dived deep into the lake's waters, with Houarn still holding on!

The swan took Houarn to an underwater palace, built of shimmering sea-shells and crystal. A Groac'h[1] [Grow-ackh] lay on a golden bed – young, smiling, beautiful. Her long black hair was braided with coral; sea-green robes of silk were wrapped around her. Houarn had heard warnings about the Groac'h, but the sight of her made his heart beat wildly – and he forgot all about Bellah.

'Welcome!' the Groac'h said sweetly. 'I love handsome young men! But why have you come to see me?'

'I want money to buy a cow and a pig', stammered Houarn. 'Then I can get married.'

The Groac'h laughed. 'Marry me instead! I'll give you half my treasure! But first, let's eat! We'll go and catch fish for dinner!'

The Groac'h led Houarn through her palace, until they reached a fishpond. 'Come lawyer, miller, tailor, singer!' she called. Four fish, all in the colours of the rainbow, leaped towards her.

1. *A mythical underwater creature*

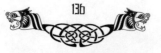

As the Groac'h cooked the fish in a golden bowl, Houarn thought he heard them talking. Was he dreaming? No! A dish of four fish was served to him, and when he cut them using the magic knife Bellah had given him, each fish turned into a young man!

'What?' Houarn gasped in fright. 'Run, run!' they warned, 'The Groac'h will get you! She turned us into fish!'

But it was too late! The Groac'h threw her magic net. Houarn was transformed. Small, green, slimy and scared, he hopped away and tried to hide.

Far away, the ring of the magic bell reached Bellah's ears to bring the news of Houarn's danger. She grabbed her magic stick and wished out loud, 'Rescue him!'

Brave Bellah held on tight as the stick became a horse, then a deer, then a bird, and soared high into the sky. It carried her to a cliff-top, where a tiny, hairy, wrinkled man was waiting.

'At last!' he cried. 'A clever girl to save me! The Groac'h was my wife; she's aged me, shrivelled me and trapped me. If you can rescue Houarn, that will set me free!'

'You must dress up as a handsome lad, and make the Groac'h fall in love with you. Then you must steal her magic net...'

'Just a minute!' said Bellah, 'How will this help my Houarn?'

The tiny man begged, 'Please believe me!' Full of fear but determined, Bellah donned her diguise, and asked the stick to carry her to the Groac'h's palace.

The Groac'h was delighted. She'd never seen such a fine lad! She invited Bellah to dinner. 'Let's have fish', she smiled. 'Come, this way, to the pond!'

Then Bellah spotted the lucky knife – Houarn had dropped it. Quickly, and secretly, she put it in her pocket.

Bellah begged the Groac'h to let her catch the fish. The Groac'h laughed, 'It won't be easy!' But, still laughing, she handed Bellah the magic net – and Bellah threw it over her!'

'Now! Be your true self!' Bellah commanded, as the Groac'h writhed and struggled. Groaning, the Graoc'h lost her beautiful shape and became a squat, squalid monster. Bellah threw the squirming little beast into a hole in the ground, which she blocked up with a boulder, just to make sure.

Next, Bellah saw hundreds of fish leaping and flapping towards her. 'You've saved us! You've saved us!' they shouted. Then she spotted Houarn. Still green and tiny, like a frog, he crouched on the floor beside her.

'My love! Is that really you?' Bellah cried, touching him with the knife from her pocket. In an instant, the real, human Houarn stood beside her, hugging her tightly and beaming with joy.

'We mustn't forget our friends here!' Bella said, and held the knife out to touch the remaining fish, who all turned back into men. Then, all of a sudden, the Groac'h's husband appeared – no longer shrunken and hairy. 'I'm free at last!' he yelled. 'Now, please, take your reward!'

Houarn and Bellah went home, loaded with half the Groac'h's treasure. They bought a big farm for themselves and some land for the men. There, they all lived very happily – and never went near the lake again.

Woman of Flowers

Out of nowhere, and as if by magic, a baby boy was born to Arianrhod [Ar-ee-ann-hrod], daughter of Don, the kindly, generous, mother goddess. But Arianrhod was bitter, and hated her son. She cursed him three times over. She swore that he would never have a name, unless she gave it to him. He would never have weapons, unless she armed him. And he would never have a human wife, unless she chose one for him.

Soon Arianrhod's brother, Gwydion [Gwid-ee-on], took the boy away from her and cared for him most kindly. He, too, knew magic, and he used it to break the power of Arianrhod's curses.

One day, he showed Arianrhod the little child – in disguise – playing with stones, and throwing them. 'That fair-haired one has a good aim!' she said.

'That's tricked you! You've named him!' Gwydion laughed. 'Now he's Lleu Llaw Gyffes [Hloo-Hlaw-Giff-ess] – the Bright One with the Skilful Hand!'

Next, Gwydion smuggled Lleu – disguised again – into Arianrhod's castle. He used his

magic to surround it with fierce, warlike invaders. Frightened, Arianrhod handed out swords and shields to everyone in the castle. Now Lleu had weapons!

To make a wife for Lleu, Gwydion wove blossoms of meadowsweet, oak and broom. He named his creation Blodeuwedd [Blod-doo-with], the Woman of Flowers. She was lovely, delicate, fragrant. Lleu was delighted with her.

But, like flowers that fade after they are picked, Blodeuwedd's sweet nature withered. She became evil, unpleasant and rotten. Lleu often went hunting and fighting, leaving Blodeuwedd alone in his castle. While he was away, she fell in love with a young lord, called Goronwy [Gorr-on-wee].

'I want to do away with your husband and marry you!' sighed Goronwy, in despair. 'But we all know that Lleu is protected by his uncle Gwydion's strong magic!'

'There must be a way to kill him,' Blodeuwedd schemed. 'I'll find out. Leave it to me!'

When Blodeuwedd welcomed Lleu home, she told him that she was afraid that he'd had an accident.

'Blodeuwedd, my love,' Lleu said, cheerfully. 'Remember Gwydion's magic! I can only be killed if I'm not on foot and not on horseback, and not in a room and not out of doors!'

'How can that possibly be?' asked Blodeuwedd, trying to sound sweet, puzzled and innocent.

'Well, here's one way, I suppose,' said Lleu, thinking aloud. 'Though I don't know why you're so curious! I could stand with one foot on a big strong goat, and one on the bath in the courtyard. The bath is not a room – just a tub with a roof over it. If you want to see, I'll show you what I mean tomorrow!'

Yes! You've guessed what happened next! Blodeuwedd told Goronwy, and he found a place to lie in wait, ready to kill Lleu with his spear. Lightly, Lleu hopped upon the bath and placed his other foot on the goat. With Lleu at his most vulnerable, Goronwy let the spear fly!

Blood poured from Lleu's dreadful wounds. But he didn't die! He changed into an eagle, and flew, dripping blood, high into the sky!

Gwydion soon found the wounded eagle, and nursed it back to health. He soon

changed Lleu into human shape again, with his aim and his throwing arm just as good as ever, if not better!

Lleu killed Goronwy, who was cowering behind a rock, by hurling his spear right through it. And Gwydion changed Blodeuwedd into a ghostly, shadowy, screech owl – a bird hated by Celtic peoples.

You can still see her sometimes, flying alone through the cold, dark, night, shunned by all other living creatures.

THEY SET
SAIL WITH
FRESH WINDS
AND FAIR
WEATHER,
AND HOPE
BURNING IN
THEIR HEARTS

CHAPTER 7

*The Voyage of Bran,
son of Febal*

The air was full of it — the most wonderful sound that Irish prince Bran Mac Febail [Bran Mac Fee-bal] had ever heard. To call it music was not enough. No, it was something greater — and much more powerful. Its sweetness enchanted him. He had no choice — he must sit down, just

where he was in the woodland clearing, and simply listen.

Bran sat, and soon fell asleep. When he woke, he found a beautiful silver branch on the grass in front of him. It came from an apple tree, and it sprouted crystal blossoms.

Puzzled, Bran went home to his father's royal palace. That night, a strange woman appeared among the guests in the hall. After the meal was over, she sang and sang – about the land of the magic apple tree.

The land of the magic apple tree was a perfect kingdom. There was no hunger, no sickness and no suffering. No loss, no sorrow, no despair. There were no wars. It was summer all year round, a time of peace and plenty. Ripe fruits were always ready to harvest; the barns were always full of grain. Animals provided delicious meat to eat, then reappeared as if unharmed. The days were for pleasure – hunting, dancing, playing games. The nights were for feasting and loving.

To Bran, it seemed as if the woman sang to him alone. 'Come!' her voice trilled gently. 'Join us! Join us! Take a boat and sail across the sea. Head on westwards over the ocean.'

'There are three times fifty islands in Tir nan Og [Tear-nan-Ogg],[1] all hidden under the water. You will find me and my many lovely friends on the Island of Women.'

Bran called all his friends and foster-brothers and described what he had heard. 'Who will sail with me?' he demanded. The young men eagerly volunteered.

They set sail with fresh winds and fair weather, and with hope burning in their hearts. As they headed west, far west, towards the setting sun, a giant – no, a god! – approached them. Through the sunset rays they saw Manannan Mac Lir [Man-an-an Mack Lear], lord of all the oceans. He rode a chariot pulled by swift white horses; the sea-green swell was his clothing. Sea-pigs (or dolphins as we know them) leaped beside him; his hair trailed pearls and seaweed.

'Look down into the water!' the god commanded. 'See! A beautiful meadow! There! Kings and chiefs are riding chariots through those flowers...' He realised something and stopped. 'Oh! But of course! You're still alive! To you, they'll be invisible.'

1. *Land of the Forever Young, a name for the Celtic Otherworld – or, rather, the happy, delightful, part of it*

He thought for a moment. 'Is one of you called Bran?' Manannan's voice boomed above the splashing waves. Bran bravely made himself known. 'Then listen, and I'll sing your future! You'll be the father of a fine son, and he'll be one of Ireland's greatest warriors.'

'But for now your life must take a very different course. Sail on west! Sail on!'

Manannan and his horses plunged beneath the waves. Bran watched, dazzled.

'Land ahoy!' the lookout cried. 'An island! With people!' But the closer they sailed, the stranger the island and its inhabitants seemed to be.

'Ho ho!' the islanders said, as Bran's ship came close to the shore. 'Ha ha! Tee hee!' They held their sides, laughing fit to burst, then making faces, pointing at the crew.

'Who'll go ashore?' Bran asked, rather crossly. 'We must find out what they think is so funny.'

One of Bran's sailors leaped over the ship's side, and waded through the water. But as soon as he set foot on the island's sandy beach, he also began to laugh wildly.

'I don't like this!' Bran said, in alarm. 'Set the sail! Man the oars! We're leaving!'

As they sailed away, Bran did not know what to think. Had the singing woman tricked him? What was going on? Where were they? And where were they heading?

'Land ahoy!' the lookout yelled again. 'See there! Another island!'

This time, Bran approached the island very slowly indeed. He could see crowds on shore, watching, waiting. They all seemed to be women, smiling and beckoning and waving at him. Bran tried to ignore them, but one threw a rope towards him. Without thinking, Bran stretched out his hand...

The woman's rope wrapped around Bran's outstretched fingers. Nothing would remove it! Bran was trapped! He felt weak, foolish and powerless. Gently, smiling all the time, the woman hauled Bran onto the island.

Bran needn't have worried. All the women on the island were pretty, kindly and made him very welcome. Bran and his men spent a wonderful year with them, feasting and dancing. At least it felt like a year.

At last one of Bran's crew – Nechtan [Neck-tan] was his name – began to grow

very homesick. So they said goodbye and sailed away. 'Be careful!', the women warned them. 'Go and see your families and friends – but whatever you do, don't leave the water!'

They sailed back safely, blown by a west wind. But somehow Ireland looked different. And why were so many strangers on the quay?

Longing to see his family, Nechtan leaped ashore. His body turned to dust and ashes.

They say that Bran's crew were horrified, They realised that they were all hundreds of years old, and headed straight back out to sea. I don't know whether this is true. But if you meet their boat, forever trapped out on the western waves, then you can ask them.

KATE COULD NOT BE STOPPED BY DOORS OR LOCKS AND KEYS

CHAPTER X

Celtic Survivals[1]

Katell Gollet
[Kat-elle Goll-ay]

ad Kate! Wild Kate! Dancing Kate! She was sixteen, proud and headstrong, and longed to be free.

Katell – or Kate – lived with her uncle, the lord of a fine castle in Brittany. He hated her wild

1. Elements of ancient Celtic myths, such as magic streams and plants, invisible spirits and wild dancing that leads to another world, have survived in many folk-tales from lands where the Celts once lived. So have Celtic festivals, especially Samhain (now Halloween). This chapter contains a few folk-tale examples.

ways, and planned to marry her to the first man who would take her. Naturally, Kate did not want this, so she made a plan. She declared she would marry the first man who could dance with her for twelve hours without stopping.

Many young men tried, but Kate danced so fast that they all collapsed – sick, dizzy, and exhausted. Kate's uncle said they were 'Feeble!' or 'Worthless!', and had them killed. But so many good men died this way that Kate's uncle decided to stop her dancing. He locked Kate in his castle tower. There she could do no harm!

But Kate could not be stopped by doors or locks and keys. She somehow escaped and found a new partner. Together, they danced day and night, night and day, crazy with love and joy and freedom. Eventually the musicians grew tired and went home, so Kate called up spirits from the Otherworld to make music for her!

Kate and her partner danced and danced to their magic tunes, all the way to the doors of the Otherworld. They danced and danced inside – and disappeared for ever!

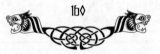

Maug Moulach (Hairy Maggie)

In daylight, you can't see her, but you know Maug Moulach [Meg Moll-ack] is there. She keeps the house quite wonderfully clean, and cooks delicious meals that float through the air to the table!

If you spy her after dark, you'll notice that Maug is small and very hairy. Like other Brownies,[1] she has no fingers or nose; her clothes are old and ragged. Some people even say her hairy hands come loose and work by themselves. A scary thought!

Maug likes to work for humans, as long as they don't try to pay her. Money or clothes would be an insult to her kindness, and to her magic. Many other Brownies have left houses where people have tried to pay them. Maug had a husband: strong, hardworking, but stupid. He liked to question everyone he met. He asked a young lady for her name.

'I'm just Me Myself!', she answered. 'Now shoo! Run away! Can't you see this pot? I'm very busy cooking!'

1. *Kindly, invisible spirits that help with the housework. Often closely linked to one particular building or family. They need regular food but are easily offended, especially by gifts of clothes. In Scotland, where this story is set, a Brownie is also known as a 'uruisg' [yoor -isk].*

But Maug's silly husband would not go away, so the woman threw her pot of boiling water over him. He limped home to Maug, wet through, scalded – and dying.

'Who did this dreadful deed?' Maug asked in alarm. 'Me Myself! Me Myself!' he replied, sadly. 'Oh silly man! You should have been more careful!' sighed Maug. 'But it seems you've only yourself to blame!' she continued, as he panted his last breath.

Later, Maug overheard the young woman and some of her friends. They were all laughing and joking. The woman told them how she'd chased Maug's silly husband away. They all thought that was very funny!

Whizz! Bang! Crash! Maug's three-legged kitchen stool shot through the air as fast as a bullet! Maug's aim was excellent – she never missed. After all, she'd had plenty of practice at mealtimes. Her target lay on the floor, dead.

The woman's friends could not see Maug, but they all heard her, quite clearly.

'You'll not kill any more men!' Maug shouted. 'You'll not kill any more husbands!'

And, after the funeral, they all agreed: it's never wise to upset a Brownie!

The Old Woman who Drowned a Valley

This myth explains how Loch Awe, a deep lake in the Highlands of Scotland, was created – accidentally!

Samhain! [Sav-ahn] It's a magic night – thrilling and terrible! The gates to the Otherworld open wide. Things stranger than our dreams rush through, to taunt us, tease us, tempt us. Samhain is also the time when the Summer Sun dies, and is buried. The cold, pale Winter Sun shines instead, and his chilly daughter, the giant Cailleach Bheur [Call-ee Vaar – meaning old woman, earth-goddess, hag], wakes from her sleep to greet him. Grim, gaunt and blue-faced, she strides through the land, shrivelling plants with her icy breath and scattering soft, freezing snow.

In her huge hand, the Cailleach Bheur holds a green holly-tree – always the sign of witches. She herds wild red deer – shy, sly, fickle, fairy cattle – and shelters under sharp, thorny gorse[1] that brings death into houses. She carries great boulders in her grey, tattered skirts, and drops them anywhere to

1. *A very prickly bush that stays green all year round; traditionally, it was unlucky to bring it indoors.*

make mountains. She hunts alongside hungry forest wolves, and swims with fish in icy waters. She makes wild winds whip, howl and whirl, and waterfalls roar and tumble. Like winter itself, the Cailleach Bheur can be merciless and destructive.

Once, a sparkling stream flowed from the high Ben Cruachan [Croo-can] mountain into a valley far below. Butthe Cailleach Bheur dammed the stream every night, and its waters stopped flowing. Each dawn, she took the dam away; the stream bubbled up, bright and fresh. In the valley, farmers offered her treasures to persuade her to send the water they depended on to live.

But then, one miserable winter night, Ben Cruachan started shaking and rumbling. After a long day leaping with the goats over crags, the Cailleach Bheur was snoring! Exhausted, she'd fallen fast asleep, and forgotten to dam the stream. It flowed on and on, fast and free.

By daybreak, shining waters covered the land for miles around. There was nothing else to be seen. The farmers and their families were all drowned. The Cailleach Bheur had flooded the valley!

The Green Children

Who were they? Where did they come from? The Green Children had everybody puzzled!

The two children – a boy and a girl - were like normal people, but green. They appeared quite suddenly, long ago, close to a hole in a hillside. They seemed very hungry but refused all food until a farmer brought them beans – fresh and green, of course.

For weeks, they lived on beans until the green boy sickened and died. After that, the green girl started to eat white milk, brown bread and red meat, and slowly lost her green colour. She learned to speak, and began to talk about the land where she once lived. Everyone there was green, she said, and it was dim and dark, like twilight.

She recalled how she and her brother had been herding sheep one day and wandered into a cave. From deep inside, they'd heard a sound – church bells – far, far away. They'd followed the bells, until they saw a bright light glowing. They had nervously tiptoed closer and closer to the light. Finally, they stumbled into this sunlit world, lost, dazzled and astonished.

What does this story say? Read it again, and start thinking! Green is the Celtic colour of death. Beans were the food of the Celtic dead.

The Glashtin

This story comes from the Isle of Man, an island in the stormy seas between north-west England and Ireland.

He's handsome, he's charming – and he'll eat you alive! Beware, girls, oh beware!

You may see the Glashtin as a wild horse in the waves, with his long mane streaming behind him. You may spot him trotting across bottomless bogs, or lurking in deep, dark ditches. But, most likely, you'll meet him as a fine young man, with a smile to melt your heart and the promise of love in his warm, caring eyes.

Fisherman Quayle [Kwayl] had just one child, a daughter named Kirree. He hated to leave her alone but he had fish to sell, and so, one day, he set off for market. He shut their cottage door and warned her not to open it to anyone except him.

Kirree was happy, but after dark a savage storm sprang up and scared her. Hail hammered on the roof above her head, and roaring winds rattled the shutters.

Where was her father on this wet, wild night? Safe, she hoped, and sheltering. She

fed the chickens, put more wood on the fire, and sat down to wait for him.

At last, at midnight, Kirree heard footsteps outside, and a strong hand at the door, knocking. 'Father!' she cried. 'is that you home, safe and sound?' She thought she heard a man's voice answering, but the wind blew the words away.

'Come in!' Kirree said, quickly opening the door. 'Come and get warm and dry!'

But a dripping stranger, not her father, stepped into the cottage. He was young, handsome, smiling.

'Sun and Moon save me!' thought Kirree. 'But he doesn't look dangerous.' Speaking foreign words, the stranger thanked Kirree – then lay by the fire and was soon asleep.

'I'm tired, too!' Kirree thought. 'But I must stay awake! So let me look at this stranger! What long arms and legs he has! What a broad chest and strong back! And what thick, black, curly hair!'

Then Kirree's eyes went dark and she gasped for breath. The room swirled dizzily all around her.

'NO!' she gasped. 'It isn't! It can't be!' She'd seen pointed horse's ears among

those curls – the sleeping stranger was a Glashtin!

Kirree was far too scared to think. She sat stone-still, frozen with horror. She knew the Glashtin had come to drag her out to sea. Then, in the waves, he would eat her.

At last, Kirree began to breathe again – though her heart was still pounding wildly. She tried to remember something about the Glashtin's powers. That's right – they faded at daybreak! If she could keep the stranger sleeping until dawn, she might just be able to escape him.

Kirree sat as quiet as she could for hours and hours. But the blazing and crackling of the fire in the storm woke the stranger up. He sat up, stood – and began to walk towards Kirree!

What could Kirree do to save her life? All she could manage was a scream: 'Aaaaarrrggghhhheeeeeeeee!' The noise woke all her chickens. They saw it was daybreak, and started to crow. The Glashtin's evil powers began to weaken! The storm he'd sent stopped, and fisherman Quayle staggered in, shivering, soaking, exhausted.

With a whoosh and a swish, like a furious horse twitching its tail, the Glashtin disappeared…until the next time.

The Chariot of Death

What's that noise? Can you hear it? A horrid, grating sound, like rusty iron wheels on a chariot. There's a thud and thump, as well, like a heavy load of stones rumbling along the road.

There, now! Don't you worry! Those old stories might not be true! That rusty chariot might not belong to Ankou [An-koo], the Death-Snatcher. And those rumbling stones may not be the hearts of the newly dead that he's carrying – but they *might*.

Many people swear that Ankou's always around. Tall, gaunt, ghostly, just a skeleton with long hair, he's wrapped in a bloody shroud and has eyes like burning candles. He carries arrows to shoot his victims, and a scythe – sharpened on human bones – to cut them down.

They say that hearing Ankou's chariot means that death will come to the family. No-one can escape him. Seeing or speaking to Ankou is another sure sign of doom.

You've heard about blacksmith Fanch Floc'H [Fankh Flockh], who worked until after midnight? Driving out of the dark in his

chariot, Ankou asked Fanch to mend his broken scythe.

Fanch agreed – and died at dawn.

FINDING OUT MORE

If you haven't quite had your fill of Celtic warriors, beautiful goddesses and devious monsters, don't worry! There's a whole world of information out there. On the following pages you'll find brilliant books, wonderful websites and some amazing places to to visit.

Information books about the Celts

Peter Chrisp
On the Trail of the Celts in Britain
Franklin Watts 2000
ISBN 978-0749638191

Fiona Macdonald
Find Out About The Celts
Southwater 2002
ISBN 978-1842156933

Hazel Mary Martell
Celts (Britain Through the Ages)
Evans 2003
ISBN 978-0237525750

Hazel Richardson
Life of the Ancient Celts
Crabtree 2006
ISBN 978-0778720454

Tom Tierney
Celtic Fashions (Dover Coloring Book)
Dover Publications Inc. 2002
ISBN 978-0486420752

Stories based on Celtic myths

Alan Garner
The Wierdstone of Brisingamen
Collins Voyager New Edition
ISBN 978-0007127887

Alan Garner
The Owl Service
Collins Voyager New Edition
ISBN 978-0007127894

Rosemary Sutcliffe
Warrior Scarlet
Farrar, Straus and Giroux Inc 1974
ISBN 978-0374482442
(other editions may also be available)

Graham Howells
Merlin's Magical Creatures
Gomer Press 2008
ISBN 978 184323 902 4

Collections of Celtic myths and legends

Eoin Neeson
Celtic Myths and Legends
The Mercier Press 1998
ISBN 978-1856352222

Rhiannon Ifans
Tales from the Celtic Lands
Y Lolfa Ltd, 2002
ISBN 978-0862435011

Gwyn Thomas
Tales from the Mabinogion
Y Lolfa Ltd, 2006
ISBN 978-0862438975

Websites about the Celts

http://resourcesforhistory.com/

http://www.bbc.co.uk/wales/celts/

http://www.bbc.co.uk/history/ancient/british
_prehistory/

http://en.wikipedia.org/wiki/Book_of_Kells

Places to visit

Birnie, Scotland

http://www.nms.ac.uk/discover_celts_romans
_birnie.aspx

St Fagans, Wales

http://www.bbc.co.uk/wales/southeast/sites/c
elts/pages/stfagans.shtml

Butser Ancient Farm, England

http://www.butserancientfarm.co.uk/

Craggaunowen, Ireland

http://www.shannonheritage.com/Attractions
/Craggaunowen/Crannog/

Further reading on the internet

Life in the British Isles during the Iron Age (Celtic-era)

http://www.britishmuseum.org/explore/world
_cultures/europe/iron_age.aspx

http://www.britishmuseum.org/explore/
highlights/article_index/p/the_people_of_
iron_age_britain.aspx

http://www.britishmuseum.org/explore/
online_tours/britain/daily_life_in_iron_age_
britain

Amazing Celtic objects

http://www.britishmuseum.org/explore/
highlights/highlight_objects/pe_mla/p/
penannular_brooch.aspx

http://www.britishmuseum.org/explore/
highlights/highlight_objects/pe_mla/t/
the_londesborough_brooch.aspx

http://www.britishmuseum.org/explore/
highlights/highlight_objects/pe_mla/t/
the_burghead_bull.aspx

http://www.visual-arts-cork.com/
irish-galleries/national-museum-of-
ireland.htm

Celtic human sacrifice?

http://www.britishmuseum.org/explore/highli
ghts/highlight_objects/pe_prb/l/lindow_man.
aspx

Celtic languages

http://www.bbc.co.uk/wales/history/sites/the
mes/society/language_celticbritons.shtml

INDEX OF NAMES

M

N

O